My Dearest Ivory

Cowboy Crossing
Book 2

Jessie Gussman

Contents

Acknowledgments

Cover art by Julia Gussman
Editing by Heather Hayden
Narration by Jay Dyess
Author Services by CE Author Assistant

———

Listen to the unabridged audio for FREE performed by Jay Dyess on the Say with Jay channel on YouTube. Get early access to all of Jay's recordings and listen to Jessie's books before they're available to the general public, plus get daily Bible readings by Jay and bonus scenes by becoming a Say with Jay channel member.

Chapter One

The auction had started.

Chandler Hudson sat on the bench outside the back door of the rec center.

He wasn't scheduled to go until last, but they would be missing him soon, worried he'd skipped out, most likely.

Still, he didn't get up. His legs were braced, and he leaned his elbows on his knees, his hands clasped between them.

Talk about getting cold feet. Although it wasn't like this was his idea. Miss Lynette, the pastor's wife, had called him with the idea of selling a month of his time at the auction that would benefit the recent tornado victims in Trumbull, which was the next town over from his old Missouri hometown of Cowboy Crossing. He said an easy yes, because hey, the auction was a month away, and for some reason, he just had the idea that he wouldn't actually have to go through with it. Who sold people? Even to make money for tornado victims?

Someone would come to their senses.

He supposed, if he were around Cowboy Crossing more often, he might have a little better idea how tenacious Miss Lynette could be.

As it was, he'd figured it out now.

Too late.

He'd taken a lot of ribbing over the last few days, mostly people joking that they would buy him. For most of the people he'd talked to, he really wouldn't mind.

His brothers had teased him that they'd buy him and put him to work on the farm.

He was between movie shoots, so he could afford the time off, and it wasn't like the work they'd have him doing would be that hard. He wouldn't be in the field picking rocks.

He'd be in an air-conditioned cab of a tractor somewhere, most likely.

There had been a few old ladies who had cackled gleefully at the idea of having him around for a month.

Even more disturbing, and probably what ate at him now, was there were actually women in their twenties and thirties who had looked at him up and down, like a horse on the block, and suggestively said they wouldn't mind having him for a month.

He wasn't under the illusion that he'd have to do anything he didn't want to—there had to be limits—but he didn't really want to spend a month bored out of his mind, at some woman's beck and call. Especially if she were a fan.

He hardly thought the situation would come up in his lifetime twice, but he made a mental note, if anyone ever asked him if he wanted to sell himself at auction again, his answer would be a definite "no."

The door opened, and Chandler looked up. A dark outline appeared against the glow of the door. A man.

"Hey," a deep voice said.

His brother, Deacon.

"Where's Tinsley?" Chandler asked, referring to Deacon's daughter, more to cover his nervousness than because he needed to know.

"She's in with Mom, watching the auction. Of which you are soon going to be a part, bro. Nervous?"

Deacon came over and stood about three feet away from the bench, leaning against the back of the building with his arms crossed over his chest, his eyes lifted toward the sky.

Chandler didn't have to see his face to know that there'd be humor there, but also a deep sadness coupled with an upright honesty that Chandler had never seen replicated in another man. Deacon had been born to be a pastor, but he'd allowed that dream to be stripped from him on the day he was to be ordained, without a protest.

Chandler would've fought, if anyone had tried to take his dream, even though he was about as easygoing as a man could be. But not Deacon. He'd shouldered the responsibility of a child, responsibility that Chandler highly suspected wasn't his, and walked away.

Didn't seem to be bitter about it either.

It kinda made what Chandler was facing now look like child's play.

"Be crazy not to be, wouldn't I? One of our brothers might buy me. I could be working nonstop for the next thirty days."

"At least you'll eat well." Deacon always did have an ability to be reasonable and to look on the bright side.

"That's true. I'm sure they'll feed me. If only because they'll get more work out of me that way."

"'Thou shalt not muzzle the ox when he treadeth out the corn.'" Deacon quoted the Bible verse in the natural way that most people breathed. Chandler had no idea how he did that. Not only did he have the verses in his head, but they came to him in every applicable situation. If Chandler had said that, it would have sounded stilted and stupid, but with Deacon, it was just as natural as hair blowing in the wind.

"Why didn't anything that you did ever rub off on me when we were growing up?"

"We're just different. Don't sweat it."

"No, I'm serious. You'd think with me growing up with you, I'd have been a little more like you."

"I'm sure you are. You just don't notice it. Sometimes I wonder if it matters anyway." Deacon said that last as an aside, and they were words that were so unlike him that Chandler jerked his head up, peering into the darkness.

But Deacon didn't turn his head to look at him, and Chandler let it slide. What would he say anyway? He was no one to give Deacon advice.

"I thought you might try to get out of this. I was kinda surprised to open the door and see you sitting here. I thought you'd be long gone."

"I said I'd do it," Chandler said, but they were just words. He knew they didn't really mean anything. He wasn't exactly known for doing what he said. If anything, he was probably known for doing what was easy.

Hollywood had encouraged the tendency, which might explain why he was here. He didn't like the man he was becoming.

More and more, it had felt like there were two sides, the good side and the bad side of him, and being in Hollywood brought out the bad side. He made a lot of money with it, and he liked that, of course. But he didn't like getting up in the morning and looking at himself in the mirror and knowing that the values of his youth were slipping further and further away.

"No one here holds anything against you." Deacon's voice was unemotional and matter-of-fact in the stillness of the night air.

"I know." They didn't because he'd done things the folks in Cowboy Crossing couldn't even begin to imagine.

Part of him wanted to do better; the better part, of course. Part of him didn't want to give up the money and didn't want to become what he'd spent his life trying to get away from.

"You know you're always welcome here," Deacon said in that same matter-of-fact tone.

"I know." He hadn't moved from his position with his elbows on his legs, and he stared at his hands, just able to see the outline from the glow of the stars.

He could come home. Of course. But what was he going to do? He'd never enjoyed the farmwork the way his brothers had. Maybe he just felt the distance from it. Sitting in a tractor, watching the machine put the seeds in the ground, endless cycles of planting, spraying, and harvesting, all of it clinical and scientifically proven to be the best and most accurate in timing and process.

His brothers would probably be shocked to find out that rather than less work, he'd always wanted more. To feel the seeds as he was putting them in the ground, to hold a shovel in his hands and feel the sun on his head.

Riding in an enclosed tractor and watching a machine do it for him, he might as well be sitting in a boardroom in L.A., talking about the latest script. There wasn't that much of a difference.

Other than the company that surrounded him, his brain reminded himself.

But no one in today's world could make a living on a small piece of property, wielding a shovel and touching the seeds himself. He wasn't even sure one should touch the seeds with all the gunk they put on them to keep them from rotting in the package.

He wanted something simpler.

Funny that he ended up in L.A. instead.

No one would understand.

He wasn't even sure he understood it himself. After all, it wasn't like he was known as Saint Chandler in L.A.

Maybe there were just some things inside of a man that were destined to never be uncovered.

The door opened again, and this time, it was his brother Clark's fiancée, Marlowe, who stepped out. "Deacon?" Her voice sounded through the night air. "Is that you?"

"Yes, ma'am," Deacon said, without shifting at all.

Maybe Marlowe couldn't see him because of Deacon being mostly in the way and with her eyes not being used to the dark.

"Have you seen Chandler? It's probably going to be another forty-five minutes until he's up, but I wouldn't put it past him to cut out. And there are a lot of people here expecting to see him auctioned. I know your parents would be embarrassed if he's not there."

"He'll be there," Deacon said. It was the kind of assurance that not even Marlowe could argue with.

Marlowe was the closest thing to a sister that they had, being that she'd been their only neighbor growing up.

"He told you he would be?"

"I'll make sure of it."

Chandler felt rather than heard Marlowe's disapproval and disbelief, but she mumbled something that sounded like "okay" and disappeared back inside.

Chandler didn't move, even after the door clicked closed. He waited for Deacon to say something along the lines of, "Now don't let me down." Or something like that.

But Deacon didn't say anything, and finally Chandler just mumbled, "Thanks."

A few seconds later, Deacon's hand, big and strong like their dad's, settled on his shoulder. "Stop being so hard on yourself. It doesn't matter to me what you do. You'll always be my brother, and that means I love you."

Chandler hadn't been expecting that. They were hardy Midwestern stock. They didn't go around talking about their feelings all the time. He had to admit it made him a little uncomfortable. But he also appreciated being accepted for who he was and not having judgment passed on what he did, which sometimes felt like the way it was in Cowboy Crossing, or what part he played, which was the way of the rest of the world.

He almost felt like he'd lost himself. He needed Deacon's grounding words.

He also appreciated Deacon's trust. Trust since Deacon didn't feel like he needed to remind him that he just put his neck on the line for his brother and Chandler had better come through.

"Thanks." That's all he could say.

Deacon pushed off the wall and opened the door with a flash of light before disappearing inside, leaving Chandler sitting in the dark, alone.

———

Ivory Haynes stood in the back of the room. She'd never seen this many people congregated at Cowboy Crossing before in her life. Of course, in her life, she'd never been invited to any of the big get-togethers. She supposed this must be what a wedding would look like. Only the people would be in church instead of the rec hall. Maybe it's what a reception looked like. She wouldn't know.

The last time she'd been in a gathering this big had been her high school graduation. She wouldn't even have been to that, except Cowboy Crossing had a truant officer who took their job seriously. Even Ivory, with street smarts that would ensure her survival in any large city, hadn't been able to shake her for long.

She supposed she owed Mrs. Davis a debt of gratitude. Not that her education had ever helped her much.

She'd been about eight when she figured out how to lie on applications and got her first job. Not in Cowboy Crossing, because everyone would recognize her. With her dark hair and eyes, she'd been mistaken a lot for a Latino in Trumbull, and by the time she was eleven, she'd been able to convince employers that she was sixteen.

If she worked the night shift, she could still go to school.

It'd taken her fifteen years, but she saved up enough money to buy a small farm of her own.

Still, she couldn't shake the stigma that came from being the daughter of the town drunk and the retired, and possibly reformed, town prostitute.

The taunts of her classmates were hard to forget.

And one taunt in particular from one person in particular had haunted her for years.

He was up for auction tonight, and although she had a lot of cash in her back pocket, she doubted she'd be able to afford him.

She wouldn't even be considering it, except someone had stopped her when she got out of her old, beat-up truck. Someone whose voice had sounded familiar. In his command to not turn around, he hadn't seemed threatening. She didn't reach for the pistol she always kept tucked in the waistband in the back of her jeans when she went out. Which wasn't often.

His hand on her shoulder hadn't been scary for some reason, and then he'd said, "Please don't look at me, that way if anyone asks you about this, you can honestly say you don't know. But I think there's someone you need to buy tonight, and I want to help you."

As he tapped her shoulder, she'd reached up, and the wad of bills had slipped into her hand.

They were hundreds. And there were fifty of them.

She could do a lot with five thousand dollars.

She didn't know how the man who handed her the money knew, though, that while she could use the money on the farm, tonight, there was only one thing she wanted to do with it.

Buy the man whose insults had haunted her for the last ten years. And make him pay.

Chapter Two

Chandler stood at the side of the makeshift stage feeling like the sacrificial lamb for the evening.

There was nothing formal or particularly organized about this auction, and people milled about, even as the auctioneer chanted in his singsong voice over the last pie he was selling.

Mr. Long, who'd managed Chandler's family's feed store for ages before retiring not long ago, walked up to him, a plate with a piece of apple pie on it in one hand and a fork in the other.

"Guess you must have matured a little since you were a kid." Mr. Long stopped and looked up at him.

Chandler figured he knew what the man was saying, so he said, "I hope I have."

"Oh, I know you have. Even three years ago, you'd be long gone." He stuck his fork in the pie and broke off another piece.

The smell of apple and cinnamon, which usually was so good, made Chandler's stomach turn. This was about the most nervous he'd been, ever. Even his first on-screen love scene hadn't been this bad. But that was probably more because the grease makeup slathered all over his body to make it look like he was sweating had grossed him out to the point where he didn't really give a flip about anything except getting through it and getting that stuff off him.

Mr. Long swallowed the next piece of pie. "I'm impressed with you, boy. I always knew you could do it, but I was never sure if you would. I used to think it was going to take a woman with a magical touch to get you headed in the right direction, but I just think maybe the Lord's working on you himself."

Chandler pulled back and looked away. He didn't need to be reminded that he hadn't lived up to his childhood church teachings. It made him uncomfortable in a way he didn't want to face, and so he didn't. It was easier to think that he was good enough and didn't need to change rather than examining his life and knowing he should.

Mr. Long slapped him on the back. "Maybe your mom will buy ya. Bet she could find some things for you to do, and she'd probably enjoy it."

Mr. Long walked away, and Chandler's eyes scanned the crowd, picking out his mom. Maybe even more than God, he felt like he'd let his mom down.

She didn't know how he felt, and she definitely didn't know what all he'd done. Maybe she suspected it, but he'd never made headlines, not because he didn't deserve it, but because he'd never gotten caught.

He shook his head, unwilling to think about it.

Mr. Humphries, the auctioneer, banged his gavel on the school desk beside him and held up the pie. "Sold!" he called out. He pointed his gavel at a middle-aged man in the back. "To Frank Audrey, for $10."

Bev Levi, sitting at the side of the stage, with the big account book open in front of her, carefully wrote the name and amount down. Her eyes lifted up, anticipation brightening them. It was pretty obvious she knew what was coming next.

As did the crowd.

They seemed to push closer, and excited murmurings swept across the room until it felt like it was buzzing.

Chandler had been a ham all his life, and he knew how he needed to school his features now. Normally, slipping into a part wasn't hard. The hard part for him was sometimes just knowing who he actually really was.

"All right, Chandler, you're up next," Mr. Humphrey said.

Chandler sauntered to the stage, confident and cocky. He gave the crowd two thumbs-up as they clapped, called, and cheered.

Normally, he could get into a part and become that person. But for some reason tonight, he felt like he was watching himself from out of his body. Watching himself walk up, watching himself look and act happy when he felt anything but on the inside.

But he was a man, and nobody cared about his feelings. Least of all him. He didn't even want to admit he had feelings.

So he sank into his part and struck a pose that an underwear model could take notes on.

"Okay, Chandler, let's keep it PG. No Elvis impersonators here." Mr. Humphries fingered the gavel in his hand.

Chandler shoved his hands in his pockets and affected a slouched, pouting look, like the latest teen idols.

He was pretty sure a couple of girls in the front were wiping drool off their cheeks. Yeah, sliding into the part was easy. Being himself had always been what was hard.

Suddenly the thought struck him: if he were being himself, how would he stand?

That was easy. He wouldn't be on the stage to begin with.

He'd always loved acting, but he loved it because it was fun, and he enjoyed making people laugh and even telling a story.

Somewhere along the line, it had stopped being so simple.

Mr. Humphries took out a clipboard and began to read. Chandler had already seen the instructions and agreed to them. They basically said that the winner agreed to feed and house him and not do anything immoral.

It was an agreement that would not hold up in a court of law, and everyone knew that it was basically up to him to keep his word and up to the person who bought him to be reasonable. He hardly thought there would be anyone purchasing him that would have any issues, and most of the townspeople probably felt the same.

The burden was on him.

When Mr. Humphries finished reading, Chandler shifted, like a model on the runway. He'd been offered several modeling gigs and always turned them down. He wasn't interested in being a clothes hanger. But he could play the part. That was what he did best.

Despite the number of people in the room, which included a lot of children, a hush descended as Mr. Humphrey started the bidding off. It quickly went to two hundred dollars and continued up.

Chandler hadn't had any idea of what he might sell for, but he was kind of surprised when, in a very short amount of time, the bids were over one thousand dollars.

Cowboy Crossing was a hardworking community, with good people, hearty and diligent. But there weren't a lot of wealthy folk. They were all very solidly middle working class.

He shifted again to the delight of the crowd and didn't really pay attention to the bidding. He knew his mom had raised her hand a few times, and he saw his brother Clark and a couple other brothers bidding on him.

That's kind of what he expected to happen. One of his brothers would win. Even his mom. If she were bidding, his brothers wouldn't bid against her except to have a little fun.

The bids kept going up until eventually it was just his mom and someone he couldn't see in the back. He was in character though, and he couldn't act like he was looking. He wasn't supposed to care. He was supposed be cocky and arrogant and sure of himself, not completely concerned that some stranger he didn't even know was going to beat his mom out and take him home with them.

His dad stood on one side of his mother, and his brother Deacon stood on the other. When the bid got up to four thousand, five hundred dollars, Deacon leaned over and said something to his mother. The bidding slowed, and at four thousand, nine hundred, his mother quit.

"I have four thousand, nine hundred. Can I have five? Give me five." Mr. Humphries's voice droned on and on in that singsong chant that auctioneers everywhere used to lure people and hypnotize them into bidding mindlessly.

Chandler almost smiled at that. His mother would never bid mindlessly, and he was pretty shocked that she would have spent so much money to begin with. Normally she was quite frugal. Living as a farmer's wife, she hadn't had much choice.

Finally, Mr. Humphries scanned the crowd one last time then banged the gavel on the desk. "Sold!"

There was a bit of a silence from the crowd as everyone craned their heads, trying to figure out who, exactly, had bought him. Chandler was curious too, but his part didn't allow him to act it.

He gave a cocky grin and looked at Mr. Humphries. "Four thousand, nine hundred. Is that all you got for me? Man, I think I need to go back to Hollywood. Their pay is slightly higher."

People were still turned around peering at the back, but the crowd laughed as he had intended.

"But they don't love you like we do!" someone shouted from the right side of the room. He couldn't see who it was, and it really didn't matter. They might think they loved him, but they couldn't, because they didn't know him.

Suddenly the energy in the crowd changed. It seemed that it was equal parts horrified, shocked, and dismayed.

Slowly, like the Red Sea, it parted, and a small figure in baggy clothing walked through the opening. A hooded sweatshirt, big enough to fit him and at least three sizes too big for the thin person that was headed toward the stage, draped over narrow shoulders, even more narrow hips, and skinny thighs.

At first glance, Chandler thought it was an old lady, since the hair falling out of the beanie almost looked white in the fluorescent lights.

White blond.

Chandler's stomach felt like a boulder that had let loose from the top of the mountain, dipping and crashing and rolling.

It wasn't a little old lady.

It was the daughter of the town prostitute.

Chapter Three

Ivory walked slowly through the crowd, her stomach clenched and shaking like a fist at a sky that refused to rain. Her chin was up. She kept her eyes staring straight ahead, ignoring the whispers and the shocked gasps as each step took her closer to the stage where the man she'd bought for the next thirty days stood with his mouth open and a horrified expression on his face.

That expression made her want to cackle, only partly because she was nervous. Obviously, the golden boy hadn't been expecting her, of all people, to be purchasing him. Those wide blue eyes and the brows that reached almost to his golden hairline shouted louder than a tractor throttle on wide open that he was definitely worried she'd live up to, if not her own reputation, her mother's.

She tried not to let the thought hurt, but her heart pinched. It always did. It seemed like one could never escape one's childhood.

She doubted she'd ever have children. If she were ever to have a hope of getting married—which she didn't, by the way—she would have to move away. But, just saying, if she did, her children were going to have a good childhood. Solid and steady.

She'd reached the stage and climbed the stairs slowly, so Mr.

Humphries had enough time to get his tongue back in his mouth and his jaw closed and a decent expression on his face to cover the horrified one that had landed there when he'd realized to whom he'd sold Chandler Hudson.

She kept her eyes blank and her face bare. She saw humor in the situation, but it also hurt, and she wouldn't let either emotion show. Years of being teased by her classmates and by people like Chandler Hudson had taught her that it was best to keep emotions hidden.

"You have to read this, and if you agree to the conditions, you need to sign the bottom." To his credit, Mr. Humphries paused before he lowered his voice and said, "If you need someone to read it to you, we can arrange for that."

In her best cultured tone, Ivory said, "I can read it myself, thank you." She reached for the clipboard, realizing her dirty hands negated the image she tried to convey with the tone of her words.

Her goats had gotten out, and she'd been putting them in and fixing the fence before she left. She'd been in a rush, concerned she was going to miss the auction completely, and arrived late.

She'd never expected to get here, be given money by an anonymous man, and be standing here now, having purchased the person she'd hated since she was sixteen.

That smirk tried to turn up again.

If the Bible verse was correct, and one truly did reap what one sowed, Chandler Hudson was going to have an interesting harvest.

She scribbled her name on the bottom line after skimming over the paragraphs. Basically, they said she wasn't going to make Chandler a sex slave, she'd feed him, and if she violated those two things, Chandler was free to go.

He didn't have to worry in the slightest about the first, and while there might not be a whole lot of money at her farm, she had plenty of food. She wasn't worried about the second either.

Mr. Humphries reached down and took the clipboard that she handed back to him. There seemed to be some concern on his face, as his jaw flexed, and he looked from Ivory to Chandler and back again.

The crowd seemed to hold its breath in anticipation.

Ivory wanted to believe Mr. Humphries's concern was for her, but she doubted it. Still, the man had too much class to tell Chandler he felt bad for him or any other such nonsense.

"Well then," he said into the microphone, sounding tinny over the makeshift loudspeakers. "Everybody, give these two a hand. Ivory Haines just bought Chandler Hudson for the next thirty days. Y'all can say your goodbyes to him if you want." He moved his face away from the microphone and looked at Chandler. "Miss Lynette said you'd be packed and ready to go."

"I am." Up until that point, Chandler had been cocky and arrogant. But those two words sounded fatalistic. Maybe he was playing to the crowd, because they laughed.

Ivory swallowed. Still making fun of her, even after all this time.

"Guess I gotta go do my duty for the tornado victims." He sounded like a martyr ready to be burned at the stake, offering himself for some good cause.

She wanted to spit in his face and tell him she didn't want him. Embarrass him in front of all these people like he was doing to her, had done to her. The temptation was almost overwhelming, and her mouth opened, but her brain said wait.

She had thirty days to make his life miserable. She shouldn't trade that for five seconds of satisfaction where she flicked her nose in the air and walked away, showing everyone she didn't want him. It wasn't worth it.

She snapped her mouth closed and straightened her already straight shoulders. She'd never been tall, and on the makeshift platform, Chandler towered over her. Straight shoulders, straight back, lifted chin, none of it mattered. She probably couldn't even headbutt his jaw.

That was okay; it wasn't a physical contest.

Although, it would be kind of nice if Mr. Humphries saw how much bigger and stronger Chandler was than her and had a few comments about her safety and protection rather than just sending sympathetic gazes toward Chandler.

"You can pay Miss Bev." He jerked a thumb back toward the desk where Bev sat, her short hair standing on end, like she'd grabbed and pulled it in frustration, pen poised over the ledger. Mr. Humphries continued, "I think you can take your..." He hesitated as though unsure what to call Chandler. He wasn't merchandise, and he wasn't stuff. "Take your purchase and move out if you've got a mind to."

The money in her back pocket burned. She hadn't even used it all, and she had some in her checkbook too. She'd gotten a hired man for the next month, and it wouldn't cost her a dime.

If she could shove aside the stigma and the hurt and the fact that the guy hated her, she could get excited about all the things that she'd get done on her farm.

He could run a chainsaw, clear out the fence rows, the goats that got out today wouldn't get out again once he helped her fix her fence properly, and he might even be able to help her with her old beehives. And that was just the start. Who knows what all they might be able to do in the next month.

Too bad she had to work with someone she hated.

Chandler hadn't looked at her, and she didn't allow that to bother her either. She didn't need to like him in order for her to use him.

On the flip side, she'd had to remind herself not to look at him, because there was a lot to admire in his outward appearance. Unfortunately, he perfectly exemplified a whited sepulcher.

Beautiful on the outside. Rotten on the inside.

Chiseled jaw. Thick blond hair. Deep blue eyes. Wide shoulders, tapered waist, narrow hips, and long legs.

Black heart.

Ivory reached the desk and stood in front of it. Even though Bev wasn't busy and hadn't been, she kept her head down looking at the book for a good ten seconds, just letting Ivory know that Ivory wasn't important enough for her to wait on immediately.

This was nothing new for Ivory. She waited patiently.

Finally, Bev looked up. "You owe four thousand, nine hundred dollars. Will you be paying with a check?" Her words were professional, her tone snotty. Again, not something that Ivory wasn't used to and couldn't handle.

"No. I have cash." She learned a long time ago that people responded to her better if she remembered her place, and so her voice was humble and soft.

The Bible said the first shall be last and the last shall be first. Ivory believed that. So the humble tone and the softness wasn't hard. The townspeople weren't mean, and she thought most of them probably didn't realize or intend to treat her the way they did. Some of it might even be her imagination. But when one held someone up in a stereotype, one tended to act toward them the way one thought about them.

What else could they do? Her mama had been a prostitute. Plain and simple. Her dad a drunk.

She couldn't really blame the townspeople for what they thought of her, and she hadn't done much to dispel their notions anyway. She hadn't excelled at school and had only gone as much as she had to. She dressed like a bum, maybe to hide behind her clothing, because it was easier to be what they thought than to try to be something she wasn't sure she really was or could be.

"Cash?" Bev's eyes had jerked up from the ledger where she wrote.

"Yes." Ivory reached into her pocket and pulled out the wad that the stranger in the parking lot had given her. Maybe someday she'd find out for sure who it was. If it was who she thought it was, Chandler would probably be pretty upset.

That could be the reason the man didn't want to be discovered.

Bev looked back down at the ledger until she glimpsed the wad of bills coming out from behind Ivory. Bev's big blue eyes got even bigger, and her perfect red lips formed a bow.

Ivory held the wad in her hand, and Bev looked down quickly, scratching on the ledger. She checked the cashbox, then held her hand out.

Ivory peeled one of the hundred-dollar bills off the wad and handed Bev the rest. She shoved the other hundred in her pocket. Maybe she should donate that to the tornado victims too. But there were a lot of things her farm could use, and she didn't have a lot of cash.

She stood patiently waiting while Bev counted the bills, twice.

"Four thousand, nine hundred dollars. That's correct." She checked the paid column.

Ivory fidgeted. At least she still had a home. It might be run-down, and it might not be worth much, but she was able to make enough money to pay her taxes and buy the groceries she couldn't grow. She reached in her pocket and pulled out the other hundred. "I'd like to donate this too. Not buy anything, just donate."

Bev's eyes went to the hundred-dollar bill waving in the air in front of her eyes, then to Ivory, like she wasn't sure if Ivory was serious, then back to the hundred.

"Okay. I've got a column here just for donations." Almost as an afterthought, she added, "Thank you."

"You're welcome." Ivory knew her voice sounded a little stilted and definitely a little haughty. She didn't mean for it to; it was just one of those walls she put up to protect herself. No one expected her to speak correctly, so there was something perversely pleasing about doing so, especially in situations where she felt like she did not have the advantage.

She might have bought Chandler, but he was among his friends and people who loved him.

She wasn't.

She didn't have friends and family.

Sometimes she wondered why she didn't find a new hometown. But new and hometown really didn't go together. And she loved Cowboy Crossing. Not everyone was unkind. In fact, no one was deliberately unkind. Not since she graduated from high school and had gotten away from the classmates that enjoyed teasing her.

But she could handle it, and it made her a stronger person. She supposed today what she went through would be considered bullying, but she wouldn't change it. Because it shaped her. If she could keep from being bitter about it, it would all be a positive.

She had kept the bitterness at bay. The only person she held any anger and resentment toward was the man who was going home with her.

"All right," Bev said. "The man's all yours. Take him home now if you'd like. Work him hard, or maybe you're just gonna put him in a corner and stare at him. That's what I'd do if I'd bought him."

Bev had a little smirk on her face, and it almost sounded like…girl talk. Ivory wasn't sure how to handle girl talk, so she didn't say anything other than, "I have better things to do than sit around and look at the likes of him."

She turned to walk away from the desk.

Yeah. Bitter. That was her.

Maybe after this month, she wouldn't be bitter anymore. Although, torturing Chandler wouldn't help her. She knew that.

There was a crowd of people around Chandler, and it looked like he was playing the martyred hero to the hilt. Everything he'd done had always been full of drama and acting. This was no exception. It hid his black heart.

The crowd parted for her, and she pushed through. She didn't stop when she reached Chandler but brushed by him, not touching. "I'm leaving. You won't need your vehicle. You can ride in my truck." She didn't even look at him as she kept walking.

"Whoa. The slave master has spoken. Now the slave must obey." His voice was dramatic, and he was hamming it up as he always did. "I'd better go kiss her boot so she'll let me ride in the front and not put me in the back with the hogs."

The crowd laughed. She had her back to Chandler, but she could imagine him giving one of his perfect, white, flashing smiles. Maybe even saluting as he turned to follow her.

Or maybe he wouldn't follow. Maybe he'd get to the door and stop. He wasn't exactly known as someone who followed through. The one time she'd been paired with him in biology on a project, she'd ended up doing everything herself. The teacher had never known it though, because Chandler was such a ham he played everyone. And she'd never said anything, just wanting to get it done so she didn't have to be around him. She hadn't wanted to work with the jerk in the first place.

Because as nice as he was to everyone else, he'd never been nice to her. She assumed she wasn't worth his effort.

She pushed the door open.

The inside of the rec hall had been busy and bright and loud and warm. The parking lot was completely deserted and dark with only one pole light shining not far from the edge of the building.

Disoriented from going from the brightly lit and busy interior to the dark and still parking lot, Ivory stood for a moment, trying to remember where she parked. Her evening hadn't exactly gone the way she planned. She definitely hadn't arrived thinking she would take a man—Chandler—home with her.

It hadn't occurred to her since the moment the man put the money in her hand, but maybe she didn't want to take Chandler home. She had tried as hard as she could her whole life to not be what her mother was, morally, and now here she was. Although she had signed a statement to keep it from going there, that might not mean anything to Chandler.

He wouldn't be interested in her. He'd been clear about that her whole life.

Those thoughts didn't give her the peace she'd been hoping for.

She breathed in the deep night air, trying to steady herself, hoping she hadn't just made the stupidest mistake of her life. She supposed she could send him home, but that would look like failure on her part, and she didn't need anything else to drag down her standing in the town. If she couldn't get along with the golden boy for thirty days, she'd probably never live it down.

The door snapped behind her, and a shaft of light broke through the darkness. Heavy footsteps. Then the door closed.

She supposed it seemed like she was standing there waiting for him, and maybe on some level, she was. But she wasn't going to turn around and look at him. She was certain it was him, because she could smell him. Not a bad way. But the same scent that she'd caught when she walked by him to the table to pay for him reached her again, only this time it was more pure, undiluted by the pumpkin and apple and other spices and the potpourri of the townspeople's scents.

If she liked the man, she would love the scent. But she didn't want to admit that the scent which reminded her of strength with a smile belonged to the man she hated.

Hated was a strong word. But she felt it applied in this instance.

"My truck's this way." She stepped off the stoop and started walking to the right. She was pretty sure she'd parked this way. Her eyes swept the parking lot, back and forth. It was full, but her truck wasn't hard to miss. There were other farm trucks there, but hers was the only one that had wooden fenders and a flatbed with wood sides. The truck bed had completely rusted off, and Boris, her neighbor to the south, who was even more eccentric than she was and eighty years old if he was a day, had fixed it for her. Not exactly fixed it, but put a wooden body on it so she could continue to run it.

Still, she didn't see it. Her determined steps slowed, and she racked her brain, trying to remember where she'd been when the man had stopped her immediately after she'd gotten out of her truck with his hand on her shoulder and given her the five thousand.

Which direction had she gone then?

And then she remembered she'd come from the completely opposite direction.

Now what? Did she admit she'd made a mistake, turn around, and go back the other way? Did she try to laugh this off?

If she were home by herself, or if Boris were there, or a couple of the ladies that she knew from town who had always been nice to her, she would laugh it off. That was her natural inclination.

But with Chandler behind her? She didn't want to admit a mistake. She didn't want to show weakness.

So she didn't. She increased her strides, until she was almost doing a power walk, and swung her arms loosely at her sides. She could own this. She'd pretend she was taking a walk before she got into her truck. One that took her the entire way around the building.

She might not fool him, but he wasn't the only one with acting abilities. He might wonder, but he'd never be able to tell for sure whether she were making it up, or whether she really wanted to walk.

Chapter Four

The confounded woman had taken him the entire way around the building.

And she'd done it at a speed that almost required him to jog, despite her short legs.

Chandler knew all about jogging and going to the gym, lifting weights and staying in shape, but he certainly didn't power walk to his car in the parking lot. He was used to a slow amble. It annoyed him that she was off to the races. Apparently taking the long way.

There were no cars around the other side of the building, and it was pitch black back there. Chandler stumbled once and bit off a curse at the crazy woman. If he broke his leg, it would serve her right —although he wasn't even sure why she had bought him or what she'd want to do with him. Maybe it wouldn't require the use of his leg.

When they finally made it around the end and came to the other side of the parking lot, they only passed about three cars before she hit the hood of a pickup.

"This is my truck. You can ride in the front if you have to, but the back is where I prefer."

She didn't say anything else, but her words made his brows twitch. In the back? She preferred he ride in the back? It only took a glance to see that there really wasn't much "back" to it.

It didn't take much thinking on his part. He put his foot on the fender well and swung his other leg over the edge, plopping down with his back to the cab of the truck.

If she wanted him to ride in the back, he would.

He'd never been hard to get along with.

He thought maybe her mouth was hanging open a little, and he suspected he shocked her. He smiled a little to himself.

He had no idea why this woman had bought him. He didn't even know her name. They'd gone to school together, and it was a small school. He remembered her from there.

Everyone knew her. Her mother was the town prostitute; it was a running joke. He wasn't sure if the rumors were true, but everyone always said her father was the town drunk.

If anyone ever said her name, he didn't remember it.

He sighed to himself as the truck motor started and the bed under him began to rumble and vibrate. Hopefully she was a good driver. Because he couldn't exactly put a seatbelt on where he was.

He needn't have bothered worrying. She drove slower than his mother.

It would have been nice to be able to talk to his mother before he had to follow the woman out of the building. He'd like to know what she thought of this situation. She'd quit bidding.

Or better yet, what his mother thought of this woman. Surely she wasn't the kind that would shoot him in the forehead.

Twenty minutes out of town, she turned off on a dirt road he'd never used. If he'd had to guess, he would have said he expected her place to be some apartment or duplex located in the lower end of town. He hadn't expected her to live out in the country.

Maybe there was a shantytown here of sorts.

That far out, there were no streetlights, no lights at all except for the glow from the headlights and the moon when it wasn't obscured by the spotty clouds in the sky. Thankfully it wasn't cold out, although he was trying hard not to shiver by the time the pickup stopped.

A ramshackle old building was all he saw in the dim light. Something that definitely needed to be torn down and replaced.

The door creaked, and the woman appeared. "This is where you'll sleep. There's a foam mattress on a ledge along the wall, the bathroom's on the far end, although there's no hot water, and there's a small kitchen sink."

When she'd spoken, he'd stretched up and looked around. This was the only building he saw in the moon's faint glow. He could see fields and fence and what looked like a shed for goats and maybe a cow. No house.

"Where's your house?" The words came out kind of abruptly, because he didn't want to be dumped off in the middle of nowhere. He hadn't thought to bother bringing a weapon.

He grabbed his duffel bag and stood, walking to the edge of the bed of the truck but not getting off. He put his free hand on his hip and glared down at her. This had to be some kind of a joke. And he wasn't thinking it was funny.

His question seemed to stop her, and he wondered about her mental capacities. Surely his family would not have allowed him to drive off into the night with a crazy person. One of them would've grabbed him and stopped it...right?

"This *is* my house. I wasn't expecting to bring you back tonight, so I'm giving it to you for the night. We'll fix something up for you tomorrow."

Three sentences. But it was like she had just read a book to him. She hadn't been expecting to bring him home?

This was her house? She really lived in this run-down shack?

But if this were truly hers, and she had no other house, she'd just given the best she had to someone that she, so far at this point in their relationship, didn't even seem to like and hadn't been expecting.

She'd given directions like she wasn't following him in.

"Where are you staying?"

Her fingers had burrowed in the material of her sweatshirt, or whatever piece of clothing she was wearing, and her eyes dropped, staring at his feet. "I think it's safer for me to not tell you. I don't know you, and I definitely don't trust you, and I don't expect you to trust me."

She slammed the door of her pickup shut and walked off toward what he thought was a small shed for what sounded like goats and cows. Either she was checking her animals, or she was going to sleep with them. Maybe both.

Whatever he'd been expecting when Lynette had talked him into putting himself on the auction block, it hadn't been this.

She still wore a beanie hat, but her white blond hair stuck out from underneath it, reflecting the light from the moon and almost glowing in the darkness. Well, he wasn't sure exactly why she bought him, but at least she didn't seem to have any romantic interest in him. That would make his life easier for the next thirty days.

Touching the rail with one hand, he kicked both feet over and landed beside the truck. Grabbing his duffel, he walked to the shed that was apparently her house.

His hand was on the door latch when he remembered he didn't know her name.

"Hey!" he called, walking around the corner of the house to where he could still see the disappearing form of the woman. "Hey!" he said again when she didn't turn at his first call.

Her stride slowed, although she didn't stop, but he knew she'd heard him.

"What's your name?" he called, determined that she would at least give him that much. He wasn't sure if he was staying. He thought it might be wise not to. But he at least wanted to know with whom he was staying or leaving.

She took at least three more steps; he wasn't sure she was going to answer him. Then her voice rang out over the night air. "Ivory."

Then he remembered. Their town wasn't that big, and he'd known her name at one time.

She kept walking, disappearing into the night without another word.

Maybe he'd offended her feminine vanity. Any other woman he knew would be upset he didn't remember her name.

She wasn't what he thought she was going to be. Maybe she was just tired.

Come to think of it, so was he. He'd worry about it in the morning.

He supposed good manners dictated he thank her for giving him her name, but he didn't. He ducked back around the corner of the building and walked in the doorway.

He felt for a light switch, but couldn't find one and finally pulled his phone out of his pocket, turning the flashlight app on.

She'd said there was no hot water; maybe there were no lights either.

But after shining the light along the wall and then checking behind the door, he found the switch. One light bulb in the middle of the ceiling came on, casting a harsh glow over the small room.

A tiny table with two chairs, a sink, a little bit of counter space, a stove that looked like it was the first one to come off the assembly line after electricity had been invented, the bench Ivory had mentioned along the wall with a foam mattress on it, neatly made. He supposed one of the two doors along the far wall was a bathroom. The other one, he wasn't sure. He strode over and opened it. It held a refrigerator and freezer.

Wow.

He wasn't sure he'd ever been in a rougher, less furnished place. The floor was wood and so were the walls. If she had a place to keep her clothes, he couldn't figure out where it was. There were no dressers or hangers or anything of that nature. No loft. Just two windows.

The foreboding that tightened the back of his neck and grabbed his stomach came back in full force.

What had he gotten himself into?

If this was her house, and she was letting him have it tonight because she wasn't ready for him, where in the world was she gonna be having him sleep tomorrow night?

But then he thought of the woman herself. He assumed she was a woman, although she was thin like a young girl. Skinny. At least that was what it looked like with the baggy clothes that hung on her figure.

He wasn't going to solve all those problems tonight, and he wasn't going to worry about it. His job was to get through the next thirty days, pay his debt to society and his hometown by helping the tornado victims, and scoot back to Hollywood.

Yeah, he might have trouble with losing himself, or finding himself, whatever. But at least he had a house there. Not some dump like this. He looked around. She must wash her clothes in the creek. There was no washing machine.

He shook his head. This was nuts. He should have paid one of his brothers to buy him. Why hadn't he thought of that earlier, instead of leaving it to chance?

Maybe he could get it straightened out in the morning. Maybe he could pay this girl to let him off the hook or pay someone to take his place.

Even as he thought that though, his hackles kind of raised. Deacon had stuck his neck out for him, and the whole town was watching to see if he was still the same person that he used to be—quitting when things got hard.

He didn't want to be that person anymore.

Chapter Five

Ivory had the animals fed and watered, the stalls cleaned out, and everything put out to pasture, in the only pasture that had a working fence, well before full daylight the next morning. She hadn't slept well. When the first gray light of dawn crept over the eastern sky, she'd been up.

It'd been tempting to go over and beat Chandler out of bed, just to be mean—she hadn't realized how deeply her mean streak went—but she wasn't sure she wanted to go there. Still, she couldn't avoid her house forever. She had to eat.

Putting the six eggs she'd gotten so far out of the henhouse in her sweatshirt that she'd slept in, she walked over to the house. She wasn't going to knock on the door; the house was hers, after all. But she didn't want to be completely rude.

So she knocked.

Two raps, and then, "I'm coming in."

She didn't have to ask permission. She could just announce herself. That was well within the rules and bounds of politeness since she owned the house.

It had to be almost eight o'clock, and she wasn't sure what exactly she expected, but Chandler was still in bed and, from the sound of the snoring, still asleep.

Now what? She wasn't sure exactly what to do. It wasn't like he was a regular hired hand where she was paying him for a certain amount of time.

Technically she had "bought" him, but there were no parameters to specify exactly what that meant.

She'd had all these grand ideas yesterday evening of all the things that they could do, things that had needed to be done for a long time, but maybe she'd just better not depend on him.

That was his reputation anyway. Of all the Hudson boys, Chandler was the goof-off, the player, the one that never followed through on anything and always took the easy way out. That's why he was in Hollywood instead of working on his own farm.

The idea of having a little help to run the place was nice, even for just thirty days, but it obviously wasn't going to pan out.

She put the eggs on the counter, grabbing a bowl and getting some butter out of the fridge.

Chandler snored the whole time she cooked them and ate them with toast and honey.

She put a roast from the freezer in the crockpot for a late supper, pared potatoes and set them on the back of the stove, ready to cook when she came in tired this evening, and thought about changing her clothes.

She wanted to. There might not be a whole lot of visitors to the farm, but she did try to keep clean at any rate. The problem was her clothes were under the shelf that Chandler lay on, and she wasn't going to wake him to get them.

The very least he could do, if he wanted to stay, was find a place for himself to sleep that wasn't in her house. Deciding to leave a note to that effect, she got a piece of paper out and was writing on the table when the snoring stopped and the man rolled over.

Big bare feet stuck out one end of the blanket, and big bare shoulders stuck out of the other end. She wasn't going to admire either. After all, the big sot was lying on her clothes, and he hadn't lifted a finger to help her so far this morning.

But her eyes didn't get the memo, not right away, and they kind of hooked on the shoulders. Not that she'd seen too many, but they did look nice. She noted the stubble on the chin, the triangle nose. Picture-perfect, everyone in Hollywood loved them. She might as well admire them while they were in her kitchen. The man they were attached to wouldn't be staying long.

Finally her gaze went to the deep blue eyes that were wide open and staring at her.

They were still a little cloudy with sleep, and she kinda figured he was trying to figure out exactly where he was and why he was there.

She'd taken her beanie off from the night before, which she kinda wished she hadn't. It was a little bit of a shield from the eyes that stared at her now.

Gritting her jaw, she lifted a brow and waited, her pen still poised above the note. The one she no longer needed if the man woke up and didn't fall back asleep. His eyes drooped, and she thought maybe she'd need to write the note after all, but then they popped wide open and shot back to her.

He swore. That word had never been uttered in her house before, and she flinched. He hadn't completely lost the small-town manners, because his mouth tightened just a little and his eyes dropped, almost in regret that he'd said the word in front of her.

"I'd hoped it was a nightmare." His lips flattened, and his arm came out from under the cover, his biceps bunching as he ran a hand over his head. "But I guess not."

She set the pen down on the table. His eyes shifted to it. "That my list of things you have for me to do today?" He yawned. "Can't a man even get out of bed first?" He shifted as though intending to do what his words applied, but then he stopped. "Unless you want to get an eyeful, you'd better leave."

"You can stay decently covered while I'm here. This is my

house." She'd never been a big talker, and typically she didn't have a lot of people to talk to. But she wasn't going to stand there mute and let him dictate the direction of their relationship. "You slept in my bed last night, because I didn't have anything prepared for you. If you're going to stay here, you can fix up your own place to sleep, and that's your first task for today. Find yourself somewhere stay."

She let the pen slap down on the table, but grabbed the paper and balled it up. He didn't need to see what she was writing. For some reason, it felt safer to protect herself from him seeing it.

She turned to walk out. Unaccountably angry. Mostly at herself. "Wait."

She stopped with her hand on the door but didn't turn around to look. She could hear rustling and movement, and if he truly didn't have anything on, she didn't want to know it.

Although his shoulders had looked nice.

She spoke to the back of the door. "If you have something to say to me, you need to spit it out. The day's half over, and I have work to do."

"It's barely past breakfast; there's plenty more time to work today. You don't have to be rude."

"Some of us depend on what we do during the day in order to survive. For those of us for whom that's true, the day is half over." She knew she sounded like a snob, and she also knew she was being mean. It wasn't entirely true either. The day wasn't half over technically, but she hated his rich-boy attitude, the one that said the world could just wait until he was ready. Obviously, his work didn't depend on sunlight or good weather. And that was fine, but she wasn't going to listen to him criticize her because hers did.

"I didn't bring food. Did you cook something?"

Taking her chances, she turned her head. He sat on the mattress with the blanket draped over his legs. Mostly decent. "Not for you. If you want me to cook breakfast for you, you need to be up when I am doing it."

"Yeah. You could've woken me up or something," he mumbled,

and he had a good point. She already felt guilty but couldn't seem to stop the unkind words from rushing out of her mouth.

"Why would I? If you want breakfast, wake up and get it."

"How about you tell me what time that's going to be, and I'll be up."

"It's going to be at 7:30. And you weren't up."

She was being petty. Of course she could have woken him up for breakfast. But in her defense, how did someone sleep through the kind of noise that she made while making breakfast?

"When's the next meal?"

"Seriously? I have a ton of work to do, and that's all you're concerned about? Eating? There are a ton of things to do today, and I don't have time to sit around and cook on your schedule."

"I'm pretty sure you signed the paper yesterday saying that you'd give me three meals a day."

That took the little wind she had left out of her sails. Because he was right. Oh goodness, she hated it when she lost an argument.

"I'm going to go through that door," she pointed to the small room that contained her chest freezer and small refrigerator, "and get some eggs to cook for you. In that amount of time, you need to be decently clothed because I'm not going to twiddle my thumbs outside while you fiddle around."

"I'll take my duffel into the bathroom and change there. All I need is for you to get out of here long enough for me to walk from here to your bathroom. And then, I need you to not come in while I'm changing."

"There is not enough money in the world to make me go into a room in which you were changing." She stomped across the room and yanked open the door to her small freezer room.

Thankfully, behind her she could hear footsteps as he got out of bed and walked to the bathroom. Her movements were brisk, her anger still fresh.

She made looking for the eggs take a little longer than it normally did, and she knew she was being unreasonable. But her years-long animosity toward Chandler seemed to erupt out of her mouth every time they spoke.

As soon as she heard the bathroom door close behind him, she grabbed the eggs and walked out. She really didn't have time to cook another breakfast, but it was her own fault. Why didn't she wake him up and make him eat or at least cook something and let it sit on the table? Cold eggs were gross, but at least she would've done what she said she would do when she signed the paper. It hadn't stipulated that his eggs had to be warm.

The butter was melting in the skillet when the bathroom door opened again.

She'd been thinking about the things she wanted to get done, and she wasn't really focused on the present, or she wouldn't have looked over.

She needed to make a mental note to not look at him. When she started looking at him, it was hard to pull her eyes away. The T-shirt was a touch too tight, or maybe it was designed to pull over his shoulders and stretch like that. His jaw was covered with stubble, and it gave him a rough and slightly dangerous look, one that curled her stomach and made her palms itch.

Her stomach and palms, and the stomach and palms of every other girl in America.

Maybe that was a negative thought, but it was enough to make her pull her eyes away. She wasn't every other girl in America. She knew what he was really like and had been the butt of his insults.

Her butter had completely melted, and she poured the eggs into the skillet.

"You're getting them over easy unless you say now you want something different." She didn't exactly mumble, and her voice held irritation, but it wasn't at him.

It was her. She'd never allowed herself to be stupid over a man. She'd grown up with her mother, after all.

"That's fine."

His toast was already in the toaster, and she reached in the cupboard and pulled out a plate. "Here. There's silverware in that drawer and a glass on the drainboard, if you want water. Anything else you have to make yourself."

"You have coffee?"

"No." She almost offered him tea, but she didn't have very much, and she really didn't want to share.

She hated what that said about her. "There's tea in the cupboard. But you have to heat the water up on the stove."

"Sugar?"

"Honey."

"That'll work," he grunted.

He moved over beside her, and that scent from last night was even stronger and deeper this morning. She hated that she couldn't stop herself from breathing it in. Shouldn't be something that she enjoyed.

She stiffened when he reached around her to grab the tea out of the other cupboard.

"Your cupboards are pretty bare."

She wasn't sure if that was an insult, or whether he was just commenting on that like he might comment on the weather. Seemed kind of personal, and considering her feelings for him, it was hard for her not to take umbrage at everything he said.

"I don't need much." There. It was neutral. Just because she could hardly stand the man didn't mean that she couldn't be nice to him.

"Most people consider coffee and sugar to be basic necessities." His tone was casual as he moved with a gracefulness a man of his size shouldn't have.

"I'm not most people." Surely he knew that if he didn't know anything else. Whatever he thought about her, she *wasn't* like most of the people he knew.

His next words confirmed it.

"No, I suppose you're not."

She didn't say anything, and the eggs were ready to be flipped, so she put all of her attention on that.

"Where exactly were you thinking that I was supposed to 'fix up' a place to stay?" He used his fingers to do air quotes around "fix up," like the concept was baffling to him.

She decided to be honest. "I really didn't think you were going to stay."

"Well, I am. Where do you want me?"

"The paper I signed yesterday didn't say I need to keep you in my house. So you can fix yourself up a place in the shed with the animals. That's where I slept yesterday."

"So you slept in your barn?" His hands stopped with the tea bag half-opened. His voice sounded incredulous.

"Not really barn. Shed. And yeah, I don't have anywhere else for you."

"Next time you buy someone at auction, maybe you'll want to consider the logistics of where you're housing them before you spend your money."

"Wasn't my money." Her hand slapped over her mouth. She hadn't meant to say that.

"What do you mean it wasn't your money?" He stopped with the honey clasped in his hand, the cupboard door still open.

Her heart had started to thump. She didn't want him to know anything about her. She wasn't sure why it was so imperative that she not tell him, although it felt like protection, like he would exploit any information he could about her. She supposed it probably wasn't true, but he had made fun of her a lot when she was younger, and then there was that one time, the one she could never forgive.

"I didn't steal it if that's what you're insinuating."

"Whoa." His head snapped around. "I hadn't even thought about that."

"Yeah. I'm sure you didn't." She almost rolled her eyes. But she scraped the eggs off the bottom of the pan instead. "Your eggs are done."

"Okay. I guess it's going to take a little longer than I thought it would to heat the water and get the tea going."

She set the eggs on the plate, along with the toast. "There's butter on the table. You can sit down and eat. I'll make the tea."

Since she was making it, she might as well have a cup herself, too. It was a precious commodity that she didn't use often. The less she went to the store, the better off she was. Tea was a little luxury that she might give herself after a particularly hard day of work, where she could sit on the porch with her feet braced on the ground, sipping and relaxing. Once a week maybe.

"After I figure out where I'm going to stay, what are your plans for the day?"

This morning had been nothing except uncomfortable for her. She didn't want him here. In her head, she went through all the scenarios she could. What would be the worst one that would make him want to leave by the end of the day?

She could have him dig rocks out of the corner piece. But she thought, especially if there were no clouds and it was as hot as the folks in town last night had said it was going to get, she might be better off having him dig fence post holes to finish fencing the twenty acres. Her animals could be grazing in there right now, if they didn't keep getting out because of the lack of sturdy fencing.

If she did it herself, she'd just pound metal stakes and string barbwire.

But if she were going to have Chandler do it, he could dig the holes and then cut trees down for the fence posts. She'd make sure he knew she wanted them sunk in at least 8 inches. She almost smiled at the thought. He'd be gone by suppertime.

Whatever he got done today would be the start of some good fence.

She had to button up her face before she turned around. "You go ahead and get yourself situated in the shed, although you can keep your toiletries in the bathroom. When you're finished with that, you can meet me in the back where the beehives are, and I'll give you your instructions for the day."

"I figured I'd be working eight hours." He slanted her a glance as he pulled out his chair. She hadn't set his plate at the head of the table, and he didn't move it.

"I don't believe the amount of time that you are required to work was specified on the contract."

"Isn't eight hours a normal workday?"

"Not for me."

"I'm pretty sure that's standard in America."

"That's fine. Work eight hours." She wasn't going to fight with him, pretty sure after eight hours of digging fence post holes through that big, rocky field, he'd be gone anyway.

Chapter Six

Chandler stopped and wiped the sweat off his brow. He couldn't believe it was only three o'clock. He felt like he'd been working forever.

Last night, as he lay in bed, he'd wondered how he was going to get to the gym. He couldn't show up to the next movie set looking like he'd done nothing for the last thirty days. It wasn't exactly an action flick—it was a romantic comedy. But he still needed to look the part of a Navy seal who'd been hired to be the bodyguard of a millionaire's son, who lived with his mother, a brain surgeon.

The brain surgeon was his love interest and the highest-paid actress in Hollywood. It was sure to be a blockbuster hit. Especially since it was scheduled to come out around Valentine's Day. It was the most romantic movie he had done to date and also the one with the highest expectations. The star power alone could carry it. There was no question it would be good.

After what he'd done today, though, the gym was the furthest thing from his mind. After pounding the hole digger into the rocky soil all day, he certainly didn't need any weights.

He stopped, leaning the handle against his shoulder, lifting his hat to wipe his brow, and looking back across the line of holes that he'd dug through the field. Exactly eight feet apart and eight inches deep. Every one of them.

Shoving his hat back down on his head, he looked toward the other end and almost laughed. He wasn't even halfway done. The rocks in this field were outrageous, and he wondered how in the world Ivory would've gotten these fence holes dug if it hadn't been for him. Not that she was helpless, but she was about half his size. It would've taken her all summer to do the holes.

At his family's farm, they would have used a hole digger attachment on their skid loader and had this done by now.

If Ivory had a skid loader, he had yet to see it. He assumed she couldn't afford to rent one nor a hole digger to go with it.

He looked across the hollow to the hill on the other side where she stood with her white bee uniform on, doing something with the brown boxes there. He assumed they were hives, although they'd never kept bees on his farm and he'd never been around it much.

She seemed pretty set on working with them, and he supposed it was safe enough. At least for him, since he was far enough away that they shouldn't bother him.

Two more hours. His arms felt like they were about to drop off, his hands burned, and he was dying of thirst, but he only had two more hours before he could quit. He sure hoped they were doing something for supper, because his breakfast had worn off a long time ago. She had said something about breakfast being late so there wouldn't be a lunch, but when he reminded her she'd agreed to three meals a day, she'd thrown together a sandwich for him to take to the field with him. Peanut butter and jelly.

He had eaten that at ten o'clock and been hungry ever since.

By the time the next two hours were done, he was ready to drop in place. It was actually 4:59 by his cell phone when he dropped the post hole digger where it stood and started walking toward the shack that Ivory called her house.

She was still at the beehives and, from what he could tell as he'd watched her during the day, seemed to be taking them apart and putting them back together. He wasn't sure exactly what she was accomplishing by doing that, but she'd been working hard at it all day.

He'd been back at the shack with his hands washed and sitting on the porch with his third cup of water in his hand, and she still hadn't arrived.

His whole body ached, but he stood and walked around the shack, looking up the hill. She was still there. Working.

Maybe she'd been serious about working until dark. That was like another three or four hours. Surely she wasn't going to work that long.

But at six o'clock, he decided yes, she was.

There was no TV, and he did not cook. But he was also tired of sitting on the porch. The signal for his phone wasn't very good, although he could use it. He wasn't used to having to wait forever for anything to load.

A little voice inside his head said, *You could text your mom, she'd come pick you up. Or your brothers. They'd make fun of you, but they'd come.*

He flipped his phone end over end in his hand. His stomach growled and cramped. His hands burned; the blisters that he'd had after one hour of work had long since popped, and new ones had formed. They bled in a couple of places. The sharp pain traveled up his arms to his elbows and squatted there, pinching.

The idea of leaving was tempting. He didn't want to stay. Could hardly stand the thought of twenty-nine more days like today.

His legs and back ached, and now that he wasn't thirsty anymore, all he wanted was to eat and fall into bed.

Except he didn't have a bed.

He wanted to throttle Lynette, but it wasn't her fault. He was the idiot who had agreed to it. She just came up with the idea.

He kept flipping his phone, feeling like the roll and flip was the way his mind was working. Should he stay? Should he leave? Yes. No.

Finally, he decided he could at least go shower.

———

Ivory set the last super back in the beehive and closed up for the day. She was a little late this year getting things set up, but for a little bit of work and a little bit of a drive heading to Springfield, she could sell her honey and make a nice, tidy profit on it. It wasn't something that took a lot of money for her to invest on the front end, and most of what she made was profit.

It was definitely worth her effort, even in spring when everything demanded her attention.

Unlike a lot of the other ventures on her farm. She only had so much time and could only do so much.

Plus, she loved working with bees.

She noticed Chandler quit at five, like he said he was going to. It irritated her in a way she couldn't explain, but she couldn't blame him. She'd had plenty of time to think all day, and an eight-hour workday for him seemed reasonable. It wasn't his farm and wasn't his business. She couldn't expect him to work like it was.

On the other hand, she shouldn't have to cut him any slack.

In fact, the more she thought about it, the more she thought she'd been right this morning that it would be better if he left. He had gotten a lot done today and hadn't messed around, much to her surprise. But still, the stress that she had keeping an eye on him had kept her from getting as much of her own work done.

All right. If she were being honest, she'd watched him just because she loved watching him. He caught her eye and held it. The beehives were far enough away she couldn't see the ripples of muscle under his shirt, but she just loved the languid moves, the sure confidence, and for some reason, especially the idea that there was someone else on the farm working beside her.

It was a new feeling, and she really liked it.

Of course Boris had been there at times, but that was slightly different. Boris was more like a beloved father, and he would help her with anything, but he wasn't necessarily a teammate. He had his own farm and his own life.

Of course, Chandler did too.

Chandler was a distraction she didn't need. It had been a bad idea from the get-go, and she was going to take care of it. Right now.

After removing her suit, she set her equipment in the shed and made sure everything was in order.

It was about two hundred yards to the shack she lived in. A beautiful walk this time of year. Missouri really showed off in the spring, with the bright green grass, yellow and purple wildflowers, and stunning blue sky.

She enjoyed the walk, thinking that she'd love to build a real house, and she was putting money back for it, but unless things changed in a major way, it would be years before she could afford it.

She was happy with what she had, but she could look at it through Chandler's eyes and see it for the dump it was. Weathered boards, no furniture, a bed that was just a mattress on top of the chest. She washed her clothes in the creek, and come winter, she didn't wash them much at all. She was alone enough that nobody cared.

Of course he thought she was a bum. He thought that or worse before he'd even seen the shack or farm.

She reached the house and yanked the door open, intending to tell him that as soon as she fed him, he was leaving.

He stood outlined in the doorway of the bathroom, in jeans and a clean T-shirt. He hadn't shaved his beard, and his hair was wet and perfectly mussed. His feet were bare.

Ivory's tongue stuck to the roof of her mouth, which opened and closed like a fish on dry land.

Why could she not get words out of her mouth?

It was another reason that he needed to go. She hated this

helpless gawking effect he had on her. It was disappointing to learn, as much as she tried to be different, she was just like every other female in the country.

She put her jaw out and took a breath, intending to force the words if necessary, however she needed, whatever she needed to do to speak.

"I'll cook supper. Then I'll take you to town. Your parents' house or wherever you're staying."

His brows shot up, and his hand, which had been running over his wet hair, hooked around the back of his neck. "Huh?"

Maybe she could have said that in a little kinder way. Too late.

"You're fired." She closed the door behind her.

"You can't fire me. I quit."

She clapped her hands together and then pointed at him. "Ha!" She shook her head. "I knew it. I knew you wouldn't follow through. I knew you wouldn't stick it out. You couldn't. You can't. You never could."

Okay. She was gloating. She tried to school her features.

"You just fired me." His eyes narrowed like he thought she'd played him. Maybe she had, but she hadn't meant to.

"You quit." Her smirk twitched at the edges of her lips.

"I'm not quitting. I'll work the next twenty-nine days just like I said I would."

"You just said you were going to quit."

"You said you were firing me."

"But I don't have to fire you because you quit."

His voice raised. "I said I'm not quitting. If you don't want me here, you're going to have to fire me. Go ahead. Do it."

She put her hands on her hips. "No. I won't. If you want off the hook, you're gonna have to quit."

"I can keep saying it until you understand. I'm not quitting."

She shook her head, hating to admit it, but she was confused. She'd walked in, determined to get rid of him, and then she was determined to prove that he was quitting, and now she was determined to not fire him, no matter what.

What, exactly, had happened?

Stepping farther into the house, she pulled her sleeves up. Her back hurt, and her feet begged to be taken out of her boots. But she needed to cook supper. The sooner she did that, the sooner she could get rid of the man sitting in front of her, and the sooner she could have some privacy and peace and quiet.

Maybe her frustration showed in her movements, because she clanked the pot full of potatoes as she set it on the stove and turned the burner on. She jerked the faucet as she twisted the handle to wash her hands. The old towel snapped and crackled as she dried her hands on it and shoved it back into its place. This was her stupidity.

Why did she think it was a good idea to have Chandler Hudson here of all people?

"Is there something I can do to help you?" Chandler had moved across the room, quiet in his bare feet, and his voice just a foot from her shoulder startled her.

"No. You can sit at the table. I'll have supper on in thirty minutes or so." She needed the potatoes to boil. Once that was done, she could mash them. "I'm taking a shower first." She could be in and out before they boiled.

She grabbed clothes, hurrying because she didn't want to be stuck with Chandler one minute more than necessary.

Chandler hadn't moved from his spot at the table when she walked back out, and she ignored him, checking and stirring the potatoes which were boiling, and grabbing some broth from the slow cooker for gravy.

After about five minutes of heavy silence, he said, "I don't understand why you're so hostile."

Her eyes opened wide, and it was all she could do not to whip around and lay into him. Did he not even remember the things he'd said to her? The hurtful, ignorant, nasty comment he had made in one of the most difficult times in her life?

But as she thought about it, she had to believe he didn't even know. She was sure she had done horrible things when she was a kid, things she didn't remember anymore. That didn't excuse it, but it did explain it to some extent.

She gritted her teeth. "Maybe I just don't like having people in my house."

"Then maybe you shouldn't have bid on me yesterday."

"That's the first thing I've ever heard you say that I think you might be right about."

"Be careful. You keep agreeing with me, and you might start looking like me too."

"I can't think of anything that could make me sadder."

Maybe she was angry. Definitely she was angry. But later, she wasn't sure if that was why she was also clumsy, or if it was just because she was disconcerted that he was there. Whatever it was, she went to pull the potatoes off the stove and drain them in the sink. She'd done it a hundred times and never had a problem, but she yanked the pot, jerking it, and boiling hot water splashed out and landed on her jeans, soaking through and burning her leg.

She couldn't help it; she screamed and slammed the pot back down on the stove. Water splashed out again, landing on her wrist. Now her wrist and her leg were burning. She danced around some, trying to pull her jeans away from her leg.

"Get them off. Get the material away from your leg." Chandler had jumped up and rushed over. His hands yanked on her waistband, trying to get her jeans pulled down.

"Stop it!" She slapped his hands away, but in the process, she hit her burned wrist against his hairy arm, and she yelped again. The scraping on top of the burn hurt even worse.

Only a few seconds had gone by, and her leg and pants were still burning. He was right, the jeans needed to go.

With her wrist and the back of her hand hurting, and maybe from the trauma, her hands were shaking, and she couldn't unbuckle her jeans.

He brushed her hands aside and pulled the clasp, grabbing her jeans and yanking them down her legs. Immediately the cool air against the wetness on her leg made it feel better. He grabbed a chair and jerked it out.

"Sit."

Taking long strides to the freezer room, he came back a moment later with two ice cubes which he put under the spicket before setting one on the back of her hand and thumb, one on her leg. The coolness felt good immediately.

Her T-shirt was big and baggy enough that she felt covered, if not decently. Although she was barely thinking about that, because the throbbing pain felt like it was coming from everywhere on her body at once and made her nerve endings feel frazzled.

"Are those the only two places?"

"Yes." She snapped her mouth shut before she opened it again and said grudgingly, "Thank you."

He grumbled something. Maybe it was "you're welcome," but it didn't sound that way. She hated being beholden to him, but she knew she was, although she probably wouldn't have spilled the water if he hadn't been there.

"Do you have an aloe vera plant?"

"No." She didn't bother to say "look around, do you see one?"

She felt like it though. But she'd been mean, and look where it got her. She didn't think God was necessarily punishing her, but maybe he was using this to get her attention. She hadn't been acting the way she should. No matter what he'd done to her, it wasn't any excuse for her to be an ignorant jerk. Because one big jerk was bad enough; she didn't have any excuse to make it two.

She closed her eyes and whispered an apology to the Lord. Then she opened them and sucked a breath in to say an even harder apology.

"I'm sorry I was unkind to you."

He seemed to study the ice cube she held for a bit before he spoke without looking up at her. "It seems like you're angry at me for something. And I'm not sure what I did."

She swallowed, somehow more conscious that her T-shirt only covered her to mid-thigh and her jeans were around her ankles. The ice cube moved slowly over her burn, and she concentrated on not letting it slip out of her hand. "Doesn't matter. It was a long time ago, and it's no excuse for me to be unkind now. I appreciate your help today and just now. You're free to go if you want."

"I told you I wasn't quitting."

"That's fine. Then don't."

He pulled another chair out and took the ice cube from her hand. She couldn't hold one on her leg and on her wrist and hand at the same time.

"I'll get this one. You do the leg. Tell me if I leave it on too long."

She nodded. Until this point, she hadn't even considered crying. This kindness, and the gentleness with which he held her hand, made her eyes want to tear up. More than anything else that had happened. She sucked in a couple of deep breaths.

"Tell me what I did. Must've been pretty bad." A vein throbbed in his forehead, but he didn't look at her.

"I thought it was." She swallowed against the brick in her throat, pretty sure she had her eyes under control but keeping them turned down just the same. "But I guess we all make mistakes."

"No. I know I was a jerk when I was younger. Sometimes I'm still a jerk. If you tell me what I did, I can apologize for it."

"You don't need to. It won't change anything anyway."

"I just saved your life. The least you can do is tell me what I did."

She jerked her head up. "Saved my life? Someone has an exaggerated sense of their own importance."

He chuckled a little. "Kidding. It worked to get your attention." His eyes narrowed. "Tell me."

She didn't want to talk about it. It was true; his apology wouldn't make any difference. And God had been working on her heart, to the point where she knew that she couldn't keep being angry about it.

Maybe she'd only figured that out just now, but whatever. She didn't want to dredge up those awful and painful memories. But she supposed he deserved to know, not because he just helped her, but because of the way she'd acted. She'd been mean. And a fitting punishment for herself in her opinion was she got to relive the pain.

She picked the ice cube up off her leg, turning it in her hand. "When my half-sister died, no one was very sad about it."

Lena had been her only sister. Ivory had loved her and had taken care of her since she was a baby. Ivory had been ten years older than Lena, and she felt like her mother sometimes.

"You mean you're mad at me because I wasn't sad that your sister died?" His voice held incredulousness.

"No." She didn't roll her eyes. She couldn't blame him for coming to that conclusion, since it took her a while to get the rest of the words out.

"She choked on a hot dog. I was eating with her, and I couldn't get it out. I couldn't save her." She swallowed, fighting back the tears. "She died in my arms. She was the only person in the world who loved me." She flexed her jaw and put the ice cube back on her leg. The pain was muted as long as the ice cube was on it. Some kind of pain medicine would be necessary, because she'd never sleep tonight with that sharp burning.

"I don't understand what that has to do with me."

"When I got on the bus the next morning, because Mom made me go to school, someone said, 'where's the other little girl that gets on with her?' and you said, 'Who cares? She's just one more brat in a world that's full of them. And we'd all be better off without her.'"

Chapter Seven

She wasn't kidding. Chandler knew that he probably actually said that, although he didn't remember. His chest ached like he'd just run five hard miles and was sucking in cold winter air in big gasps.

He could say he hadn't known. Of course he hadn't known her sister died. At least he didn't think he had. News did travel fast in a small town. But even though he knew he could be a jerk at times, he knew even he wasn't that much of a donkey's butt.

"Sorry." It seemed so inadequate. "That was inexcusably ignorant. And I'm sorry. I don't know what more I can say. I know there's nothing I can do to make up for it."

He moved the ice cube on her hand; it already was red and blistered. "We should take you to the hospital for this. Burns can get infected, and then you're really gonna be in trouble."

"No."

She didn't say anything more, and he assumed, although he did not say, she probably didn't have insurance.

"Is there anything I can do to make it up to you?"

She shook her head. And that nasty, wormy feeling just

intensified. Because she was looking down at her leg and wouldn't even look at him. He didn't deserve it anyway.

Man, he'd been a jerk.

He held her hand in his, not much bigger than a child's hand. Was it small because she'd been malnourished as a child?

He wouldn't have noticed when he was growing up. Kids didn't notice those things; at least he never had.

And now, he kind of wondered exactly what her life had been like living with the town prostitute. No dad. Or a dad who was drunk all the time. Her dad had died at some point, but he didn't know when.

Her white blond hair hung on either side of her shoulder—a contrast against her dark T-shirt.

As he sat there, staring at it, feeling awkward and clumsy in the silence, he started to realize how delicate her bone structure was, how small and fragile she looked, almost like a child. And yet she'd outworked him today.

He suspected she could outwork him every day.

He looked around the house with new eyes. Everything was run-down—there was no denying it—but it was neat.

Still, living here would be harsh, and she didn't look like she could stand up to much of anything.

"How long have you lived here?"

The last he'd heard about her, she lived in town with her mother, who had a room in the back of one of the bars in town. At one point, he thought Ivory's mother had lived behind each of the three of them. And possibly the Mexican restaurant as well. Depending on her relationship with the owner, or maybe depending on the favors she was providing the owner, making money on the side providing those same favors to others.

Everyone knew it, and everyone looked the other way. It helped that one of the county judges had been one of her biggest customers.

What a life for a little girl. No wonder she was close to her sister.

"I bought it three years ago."

Three years. Three winters. Three storm-filled springs.

"What do you do when a tornado comes?"

"I go lie in the hollow."

That hardly seemed safe, but he'd heard of people doing that. He supposed it would work.

"Can you hear that tornado siren from here?"

"Most of the time."

Yeah. Sometimes the sound traveled, sometimes it didn't.

"A phone?"

"No."

"You should. You can see the weather on it. At least know if there are a lot of storms coming."

"I just watch the sky. I can pretty much tell."

Maybe she could. He supposed that was what people used to do.

"How old was your sister?"

"She was six."

"Where was she buried?"

"Mom had her cremated. It was cheaper."

"Where are the ashes?"

She lifted her shoulder, shook her head. Her throat worked. "Mom had them put in an urn, but she had a fight with one of the men who came to see her, and it fell and broke."

What did one say to that? He supposed he could ask if she swept it up. That just made him nauseated.

"I wasn't at home. I was working. Mom just told me about it when I got back. I don't know what she did with them." Her thin shoulder lifted. "Doesn't matter. My sister was gone anyway." She moved the ice cube around on her leg, and Chandler looked down at the loud, angry red spot that stretched from her mid-thigh clear down to her knee.

Her legs were white and thin, and shapelier than he would have imagined under the baggy jeans she was wearing. He pulled his eyes away, settling them on her hand and focusing on moving the ice cube around the burn.

"How's it feeling?"

"Hurts."

"I don't know what else to do. I guess I could look up first aid for burns on my phone, but I'll have to take the ice away for a couple of minutes."

"You don't need to bother. We're doing everything we can. I probably will take some kind of pain medication so that I can sleep. Otherwise it'll be burning all night."

"I think you need to take tomorrow off."

"I have too much work to do. I can't take off."

"I'll get up. I'll help. Tell me what to do."

"I have my animals to feed yet tonight. I was going to feed you first, because I know when you're not used to this work, it's hard. I figured you were hungry." She bit her lip and said in a small voice, "I'm sorry about the peanut butter and jelly sandwich." She took a breath in then let it back out, blowing hard. "I wasn't expecting to buy you. I'm sorry. I wasn't prepared, and you suffered for it."

"Who gave you the money for me?" He'd forgotten all about that. That she'd said the money hadn't been hers.

"Someone gave it to me, but I don't know who. They told me not to look at them so that I could honestly say I don't know. I'm glad they did now. Because I really don't know."

It felt almost like a reconciliation, or a truce, and Ivory didn't want that. She didn't want to be "friends" with Chandler.

She moved the ice cube around the blistering spot on her leg, conscious of him cradling her hand, much smaller, in his. Both spots hurt equally bad. The burn on her hand was smaller in area but had bigger blisters.

Regardless, it didn't matter. She needed to be firm.

"I really do think this was a mistake. I don't know why the guy gave me the money, and I don't even know what prompted me to go through with it, but I think we gotta just admit here and now that it didn't work out, for both of us, and agree to call it quits."

He had his head down, staring at her hand where he absently moved the ice cube back and forth. She had to admit he was gentler than she had expected. Her expectations of him had not been high.

It took a while for him to say anything, and it was quiet in her kitchen; not even the ticking of a clock broke the silence. He finally spoke.

"I guess you're right. I wasn't cut out for this kind of work."

The way he said it, he sounded sad, almost like he wished he *were* cut out for that kind of work.

But she had to agree with him. "I'm sure you make a great action hero. But farming is a completely different scenario, and it doesn't really fit who you are." She tried to word her statement nicely, considering their newfound neutral ground. But basically, the man wasn't cut out for physical labor. God made him to look good, and maybe even made him a good actor, although she'd never seen any of his films, so she wouldn't know.

He nodded but didn't reply to her comment. "Whenever you're well enough to drive me back into town, I can be ready to go."

"I'm well enough to drive you anytime. I just need pants. But I think it's only right to feed you first." She shifted on the chair, a little embarrassed. The pain had dulled somewhat, or maybe she just got used to it. And now the completely bare state of her legs, clear up to her underwear, hidden only by the length of her T-shirt, definitely made her want to squirm.

She had less showing than she would if she were wearing a swimming suit at the beach, but she just felt exposed.

She cleared her throat. "If you wouldn't mind leaving for a minute, I'll get dressed and get supper on the table."

His eyes came up, and she thought she read a little confusion in them, but it was hard to tell. They were a rich, deep blue, and there seemed to be thoughts there that she hadn't even guessed at. Maybe it was her imagination, because she had trouble pulling herself away, feeling like she was caught and falling.

But he broke the spell when he glanced down, and a flash of humor crossed his face.

It made her angry.

"Just because some of us still have a touch of modesty doesn't give the rest of you the right to laugh."

That really did make his lips turn up, and she almost felt like steam was coming out of her ears.

His voice held humor. "I know who your mom was. Remember? I grew up in the same town as you. You don't have to lecture me on modesty."

Now, not only was she angry, but she wanted to smack him right in the nose. "You have no right to judge me based on what my mother was. You don't know me at all."

Her lines were trite, and she knew it. But they were the truth.

"Wasn't judging you." He still didn't seem to understand how close he was to getting socked in the kisser.

"Yes, you were. You were assuming that I'm not modest. You can make that assumption all day long if you want to, I don't care. Just get out so I can get dressed."

He blinked, with his mouth half open. Maybe he really didn't think he was judging her. But how could he not know?

"I'm sorry." He said the words slowly, drawn out, like he was trying to figure out exactly what he was apologizing for. Which didn't help assuage her anger at all. "I guess after spending so much time in Hollywood, I'd forgotten that there were attitudes like yours in the world. I really am sorry."

"Funny. You didn't say anything about Hollywood. You mentioned my mother. You think I don't know what she was? That doesn't mean that I can't be something different." She set her jaw, not wanting to say what she knew she needed to. One couldn't have someone offer an apology and not accept it.

"I accept your apology." She spit the words out, sounding more like she was saying *I don't accept your apology*. Nonetheless, she'd made the effort. Even just saying the words was hard, because she was right.

"Do you need me to do anything or get something for you before I walk out?"

"No." If her hand didn't hurt so badly, she'd have her arms crossed over her chest. As it was, she stared at the wall. Waiting.

He seemed to sigh before he pushed himself up from the table. "I'll walk to the shed and get my clothes." He stopped behind her chair, and she couldn't see him when he said, "If you tell me how to feed the animals, I'll do that while I'm out there and save you from it tonight."

"No thank you. I like doing it." She wasn't being the slightest bit gracious; she was being mean, and she knew it. She really didn't care.

He left without another word, and she scrambled up immediately, putting a loose skirt on. She also walked to the bathroom and grabbed a couple of pain pills. As soon as the ice quit touching her skin, it started burning again. By the time she was dressed, it was seriously hurting. It could end up being a long night. And she wasn't sure she would be able to wear jeans in the morning.

She would cross that bridge when she came to it. For now, she needed to get supper, get that man out of her house and off her property, and take care of her animals.

The troubles of tomorrow would take care of themselves. And she'd get to them when she got to them.

Chapter Eight

Chandler sat in the passenger seat of Ivory's old farm pickup. It was almost dark, and they were on the outskirts of Cowboy Crossing. She wore a flowing skirt rather than the jeans he'd seen her in up until that point, and he assumed her leg must be hurting, because her fingers gently rubbed her knee. Probably the skin right beside the burn.

Whether she did it on purpose to try to take her mind off the pain, or whether it was something she did normally, he wasn't sure. But the burn on her hand had turned into one big blister, filled with water, red and painful looking.

He hadn't said anything since he got in the truck and had said very little since her argument about him thinking she wasn't modest.

He'd realized, after he left the kitchen, that she was right. He had made assumptions about her based on her mother, and the way she'd been raised, and the things he thought about her in high school. None of them had borne out in the day that he'd been on her farm.

But he'd already apologized, and to bring it up again was probably overkill. She hadn't taken his first apology very well anyway.

He had his own demons he was dealing with, beside. Basically, he hated that he was "quitting." Although she'd clearly told him she didn't want him anymore. Still, she talked about a mutual agreement, and so that implied that he was on board with this too.

"Where do you want me to drop you off?"

He shifted, his head turned and looking out the window as they passed the feed mill his family owned on their way into town. "My car's still at the rec center."

"You have your keys?" she asked. He didn't know why she cared. It wouldn't matter one whit to her whether he could start his car or not.

"Yes." And his duffel. He supposed he was coming into town a little better than he'd left, since she'd let him sit in the cab of the truck, and yesterday he'd been relegated to the back.

The rain that was now coming down might have something to do with that. She wasn't heartless after all.

That was an unkind statement, because she wasn't heartless at all. She'd been badly treated by him, and he hadn't even realized it. He didn't have any recollection of saying what she said he had said about her sister and her death, but he had no doubt he said it. The pain she carried was real.

And he caused it.

He hated that.

He supposed in the last twenty-four hours he'd developed a grudging respect for her, or at least she'd shattered his preconceptions about her and forced him to construct new conceptions of her.

He noted she didn't use a turn signal or wear a seatbelt as she pulled into the rec center and parked beside his car, which was the only one in the lot.

"Do you need help with your stuff?"

It was a rhetorical question, he supposed, because he just had the one duffel.

He wasn't completely incompetent, although his hands were burning. As long as he kept them still, they didn't hurt much at all, but every time he flexed or moved them in any way, the blisters that had formed that day while he had been digging fence holes—filled with pus, and popped, and now bloodied red blotches on his hands—pulled and burned like someone was setting a hot iron on his palms.

He couldn't say anything about them though. Because she hadn't uttered one word of complaint about the big burn on her hand or the even bigger one on her leg.

Not to mention, he had a feeling that none of the men in his family would have hands that looked like his after not even one full day of using the post hole digger.

They'd all make fun of him if they knew.

Not that he thought that Ivory was going to tell anyone, but she'd probably make fun of him too. A real man didn't get blisters on his hands, because he already had calluses.

Not that anyone ever actually taught him that; it was just something everyone knew. One more thing that set him apart from his brothers and made him less.

Ignoring the burning pain in his hands, he yanked on the door latch. "No. I've got it. Thanks for the ride."

"Thanks for the holes you did today." Her words were soft, and they almost sounded contrite. Like she figured she owed him.

He didn't feel like she did.

Feeling like he was making a big mistake, and also living up to everyone's really low expectations of him—maybe living down to the expectations—he slid out of the truck.

What to say to someone whom one thinks one probably will never see again, except possibly around town and maybe not at all?

Talk to you later didn't sound right. *See ya around* didn't sound right either.

He finally settled on, "Have a good night."

He wanted to say something about her burns, and them getting infected, and taking care of herself. He didn't even know why he would care. That was new.

"You too."

If she had the same trouble trying to figure out a good note to end on, it didn't show on her face when he glanced at it. She wasn't even looking at him. She had her hands on the steering wheel and was staring out the windshield at the wipers that only partially worked, and didn't really clean the windshield at all, but just kinda smeared the raindrops on it.

With his keys in one burning hand and his bag in another, he slammed the door and ducked through the rain to his car, throwing his bag in the back, getting in the front, and shutting the door.

She still sat there, and he figured she was probably waiting to make sure he got the car started. Not because she cared, necessarily. It was a country thing. You just didn't pull away from someone until you knew they were able to get going from where they were.

So he started his car, turned the parking lights on, and put it in drive to let her know that he was now mobile.

She blinked her lights, which surprised him, and then she pulled away.

After a second of hesitation, he blinked his at her.

Delicate features, slender limbs, white blond hair, and cherry red lips. He hadn't expected those images to stick in his brain. That would've been the very last thing he would've even thought about when he followed her out the rec door last night.

But now, those were the only pictures that floated through it. And they were underscored by steely determination, stubborn refusal to be like anyone else, and a gritty insistence that she could survive and thrive on her little plot of land.

It'd only been twenty-four hours, but how could he not admire that?

Chandler thought of his parents' house; that was probably where he'd end up. But he didn't want to go home. Not yet.

He didn't even know where he actually really wanted to be. He pulled out of the rec building and drove slowly down the street to the diner.

The rain made dusk come earlier. It was only about 8 o'clock. He wasn't hungry, but he figured he'd go in to drink a cup of coffee, and that would delay his homecoming a little bit.

He paused with his hand on the door, seeing through the window that Deacon and Pastor Wyatt sat at the table in the corner. He would've turned around, but just then his brother's eyes lifted and met his through the glass.

He could hardly back away now. So he opened the door and went in.

Deacon was already standing up, smiling and welcoming, but also a little confusion on his face.

Of course, Chandler thought. They were probably all expecting him to quit, but not after just one day.

"Chandler!" Deacon walked across the diner to him. Pastor Wyatt got out of his seat and followed. "We were just talking about you and were about to come out and see you. We didn't want to interrupt supper or feeding time."

Pastor Wyatt joined Deacon and held out his hand. "All of that is true, but we also both needed sitters for our children before we could come. My wife has been out visiting and just got home."

Chandler clasped Pastor Wyatt's hand and tried not to grimace. It didn't matter; the pastor noticed anyway.

"What in the world have you done to your hands?" he asked as he looked down.

Chandler snatched it back and shoved them both in his pockets, ignoring the pain that traveled like electrical pulses up his arms and made the back of his neck hurt.

"Ha. Looks like someone has soft hands, huh?" Deacon, who would give him the least hard time of all of his brothers, smirked and slapped him on the shoulder. "Maybe you should wear gloves next time, bro."

Yeah. Gloves would've made it all better. But he hadn't even thought about it. Which probably showed just how much of a fool he was.

"What were you guys going out to see me for? Is there a

problem?" Chandler asked, as much to change the subject as he wanted to know what they wanted.

"No. We just wanted to check and make sure you're doing okay. That she's treating you good." Deacon smirked a little at that too, and that was about the most smirking Chandler had ever seen Deacon do in one day in his life before.

"I was fine."

"Then what are you doing here? Didn't she feed you supper? And aren't you supposed to be staying there?" Pastor Wyatt asked. Although his questions were probing and a little bit nosy, they didn't seem that way coming from him, because his eyes shone with genuine caring.

"We both decided it was better if we went our separate ways."

Both men froze.

"You quit?" Deacon said softly. Maybe he was trying to hide the disappointment in his voice, but he wasn't entirely successful.

Chandler's chest constricted. His breath hitched painfully, rivaling the pain in his hands.

"Want to come on over here and sit down and talk to us about it over coffee?" Deacon asked, pointing to their table and leading the way over.

Chandler thought about not following, about turning around and walking out, but he couldn't do that to his brother.

They'd barely gotten situated at the table, with Chandler around one side and Deacon and Pastor Wyatt on the other, when Amy, the waitress, bustled over with the coffeepot.

"You two boys want refills?" she asked.

Deacon held his hand up as a no, but Pastor Wyatt said, "Yes, please."

She filled his cup up, then turned to Chandler. He knew her from school, although they never really hung together.

"Chandler, saw you at the auction yesterday. You looked mighty fine standing up there on the stage." She put her hand on her hip and tilted her head. "I'm surprised to see you here."

"Yeah." Gossip traveled faster than wildfire in a small town, and a lot of it started here at the diner. He wasn't even going to go there. He didn't want to do that to Ivory.

"Well, can I get you anything? A cup of coffee? Piece of pie? We got some mighty fine pumpkin in the back there. I think there's one piece of lemon meringue left. Grandma Baker made that. It's really good."

"No, thank you." Ivory hadn't made any dessert with supper tonight, but the roast and mashed potatoes and gravy were better than even his mom's. And she hardly put any time into it at all.

It was pretty amazing, when he thought about it, that she'd made something that good after working all day.

"You boys just holler if you need anything." Amy gave them all one last look and hustled off. The diner wasn't full, not at this time of night, but she did have other customers.

"We were coming out to see you, to encourage you. But you're here now, did you...quit?" Pastor Wyatt asked over his steaming coffee cup.

"I told you, we came to a mutual decision." Chandler knew he was going to be interrogated, and he wasn't looking forward to it. But he didn't have to answer now. He could avoid it and wouldn't have hesitated dodging Pastor Wyatt's questions, but he couldn't hurt Deacon that way. Deacon had put up with a lot of his stuff over the years.

After this failure, he figured he probably owed it to his brother, especially after Deacon stuck his neck on the line for him yesterday.

"What happened?" Deacon asked again.

Pastor Wyatt had his hands steepled in front of him, and his caring gray eyes were focused on Chandler.

Neither one of them were there to hurt him or to give him a hard time. They truly cared about him.

It felt good. Especially after all the time he'd spent in Hollywood, where no one truly cared. It was all about appearances and money. At least that had been his experience.

There had to be good people in that town. He just hadn't run into any. Including himself.

"I don't know." Okay, that wasn't the entire truth; he felt guilty as soon as he said it. "I guess I was a jerk to her when I was younger, and she doesn't like me. And I think she had buyer's remorse." He turned his hands around on the table. "And I did work today. You know me." He pasted a carefree grin on his face, because he wouldn't bare his heart, even if he did love his brother. "One day of hard labor is enough to last me for the next ten years. She fired me, and I quit, and we came to a mutual decision to part ways. And that's the truth."

Pastor Wyatt nodded with a thoughtful look on his face.

But Deacon spoke immediately. "And you're okay with that?"

Chandler started to nod yes, but in his heart, no, he wasn't. He hated that he quit something yet again. Even if the lady had wanted him to.

"We just decided we were better off apart. Some people just don't rub along together very well."

"You're not getting divorced, and you're not married. This is just thirty days of you working for her." Pastor Wyatt spoke, and Chandler allowed a ghost of a smile to touch his lips. He supposed it did sound like something a divorcing couple might say. It hadn't been how he'd meant it. There'd been no relationship to speak of between Ivory and him.

He wouldn't even have touched her, if she hadn't burned herself.

With that thought, he figured he'd probably seen more of Ivory than either of those two men ever had.

A little voice in his head said he'd seen more of Ivory than any man in the town had.

His eyes narrowed as his hands flipped back down on the table, the cool tabletop underneath them feeling good on his burning and seeping blisters.

Funny how a burn hurt right away, but his blisters had taken some time to start really bothering him.

His day on her farm had shifted the way he thought about Ivory, but he realized it was probably true. Thinking back over the few times he'd seen her in town, he recalled she'd always worn baggy clothing, usually a hooded sweatshirt, except in the very hottest of weather, and often boots. She looked like a bum who had raided the closet of someone who was seven sizes bigger than she.

The image of her mother, and the idea that she was just the same, had been so permeated in his brain.

He'd been wrong.

"Is that the way it's going to end?" Deacon asked.

"It has to be. The lady doesn't want me." At one time, he might have said "lady" referring to Ivory with a sneer or at the very least an irreverent grin. But now he thought the word suited her.

The pressing together of Deacon's lips showed that he was disappointed, but he didn't say anything more.

Pastor Wyatt set his coffee cup down. "My wife has been working with Ivory for a few weeks. She's finally started to come to some of the ladies' meetings. I didn't grow up in this town, but I understand her upbringing and experiences haven't been the best. I was very happy, and my wife was happy, when she bought you." His lip twitched just a bit, and Chandler thought maybe the good pastor had been concerned about the auction taking a turn toward the unbiblical. He wouldn't have been surprised if Pastor Wyatt and Deacon had a plan B to keep that from happening.

Pastor Wyatt continued. "She could really use a hand out there, and there are not a lot of people who'd be willing to do it for nothing, because as I understand it, that's all she can afford to pay." Pastor Wyatt glanced at Deacon, and Deacon shook his head just a bit. Chandler wondered at the byplay between them.

Did it have anything to do with the five thousand dollars Ivory had been handed? Because when Pastor Wyatt said she couldn't afford to pay, that money would have been a man's wages for a few months over the busy time of summer.

He imagined that Ivory wished now she had kept the money and used it to hire someone who would actually have been a help to her.

Too late.

At least the money went to a good cause.

"I can go back out."

This was one of those times in his life Chandler wanted to take his lips off and examine them. That thought hadn't even been in his head; how did it come out of his mouth?

He had to make his lips turn up in a smirk, because he didn't want them to read too much into that statement.

It shocked him to realize he *wanted* to go back. Almost to the point of *needing* to go back.

Deacon's eyes lit up, and Chandler didn't need a crystal ball to know that was what Deacon really wanted him to do.

Deacon glanced over at Pastor Wyatt, and Chandler got the impression that whatever Deacon was going to say was something Pastor Wyatt didn't know. "I wasn't going to tell you this, but after you left, there was a big bunch of guys in the corner in the back of the rec hall taking bets. Most of them said you wouldn't last for thirty days, and more than half of them said you wouldn't last ten."

Chandler blinked at Deacon, who looked down at his hands, which were big with rough knuckles and wrapped around his empty coffee cup. His first finger tapped one tap every two seconds, just a little tell. Deacon wasn't quite as relaxed as he looked.

A little thought crept into Chandler's brain. He said the words before they had completely mulled around in his head. "Did you bet?"

Chandler would've said without reservation, even thirty seconds ago, that Deacon would never bet money on anything. He would *never* bet. It was wrong.

Deacon swallowed, and his finger tapped a little faster.

Pastor Wyatt looked over, his eyebrows up, his mouth open.

Dishes clanked somewhere, and someone laughed. The bell for an order coming up rang, and a low murmur of voices filled in the air pockets as Chandler waited on Deacon.

Deacon's head lifted, and his chin jutted out. "I bet five thousand dollars you'd last the whole thirty days."

Chandler's eyebrows shot up, and his hands fisted, sending seeds of pain up his arms. "Five thousand dollars?"

Chandler didn't need to repeat it; Deacon hadn't stuttered, and he hadn't had a problem hearing him. He couldn't believe the faith his brother had shown in him. And he let him down.

Unless he went back.

It's what he wanted to do. He hadn't wanted to quit, not really. And yeah, Ivory didn't want him, but she'd bought him, and they both signed the paper agreeing to thirty days. He had every right to be out there for the next twenty-nine.

He nodded. "That's all I needed to hear, bro." He slid out of the booth seat and stood. "You know where I'll be if you need me."

"Do you need something for those hands?" Deacon asked without getting up.

Chandler almost said no, but he didn't even own a pair of gloves. And he'd guess, if Ivory had any, they'd be way too small for him.

"Gloves?"

"I have some in my truck." Deacon slid out of the booth and walked out of the restaurant with him.

Chapter Nine

Ivory didn't know what she was expecting in the morning, but it wasn't to wake to the sound of pounding. She didn't have a clock, but the sun wasn't even up, although the gray light of dawn poured in her window. Her leg burned along with her wrist, and she was careful how she moved as she rolled in her bed, leaned up on her elbow, and peered outside.

Chandler was out in the field that he'd left last night, and he was slamming the post hole digger up and down on the ground. He must have hit a rock, which was what woke her.

She noted the gloves on his hands and wondered, for the first time, if he needed them yesterday and if he had blisters on his hands that she'd missed, because of being more concerned about the pain of his comments and then the pain of her own burns.

Regardless, she wasn't sure whether she was happy or irritated to see him out there.

There definitely was some kind of stirring in her chest and a feeling that made her lips want to turn and tilt and her heart smile. But there was also the idea that she had to deal with him.

She hoped she'd forgiven him. He'd apologized, but she'd hated him for so long she wasn't sure exactly how she felt about him.

She got out of bed and put the flowing skirt back on after taking a good look at the burn on her leg. If she wore jeans today, it would be rubbed raw before breakfast. She didn't want to go to the hospital, and she wasn't going to, but she wasn't going to be foolish about it either. Burns really were easy to get infected, and she wanted to take care.

Ten minutes later, she was walking up the field toward Chandler. There was no point in putting it off. She needed to find out what was going on.

His back was to her. She supposed since he was on her property—although what kind of logic that was she wasn't sure—she could admire him as much as she wanted to. After all, it was how he made his living. Acting was only a small part; he wouldn't be paid to be on the big screen if he didn't look good. So she wasn't the only one who wanted to stare at him.

And maybe, *maybe* she'd been a little wrong about him, or maybe he'd changed, because yesterday, he'd been a lot nicer than she was expecting.

Still, she didn't quite think his insides matched the good looks of his outside, but she could be wrong.

She doubted it.

She stood to the side, and when he saw her, he gave one last slam into the ground and allowed the post hole digger to stand there while he straightened and lifted his cowboy hat, wiping his forehead before setting it back down.

She held out the bottled water she carried.

He took it. "Thanks."

Uncapping the bottle, he drank half of it before lowering it and wiping his lips with the back of his glove.

She looked away, up the hill at the beehives where she'd been working yesterday and where she hoped to be working at least long enough to get some equipment to clean today.

"You're back." It was obvious, but she wasn't sure what else to say.

"Yeah."

They stood in silence as the seconds ticked by. Awkward silence, and neither one of them seemed to be the one to want to break it.

Finally, he said, "How's your burns?"

"They hurt. But I took some pain meds for them, and the pain should be gone in another fifteen or twenty minutes." Her eyes went to his hands and the gloves he wore. "You have gloves today?"

"Yeah."

She needed to figure out how to ask questions that elicited more than a one-word answer. "I have to feed the animals, and then I was going to cook breakfast. I was here to see if you wanted some."

"Yeah. Please."

"It'll be ready in forty minutes. Can you come down?"

"I'll be down in thirty."

"Okay." She started to turn, but his voice stopped her.

"Is this where you want me today?" His voice wasn't hesitant, nor humble, but there was a definite deference there, letting her know she was in charge. In case she doubted.

"This's fine. It needs to be done. The sooner we get this fence up, the sooner the animals can be out here grazing. The hay I'm feeding them will still be good next winter."

"I'll do my best to get it done as fast as I can. You have barbwire?"

"No. We'll have to go to town for it when we're ready."

She'd said "we." She supposed she should have just said "I," although maybe he'd want to go with her. She really didn't know anything about him other than what she remembered, and obviously he'd changed from what he was when he was a teenager, just as she had hopefully.

"How many eggs you want?"

"How many do you have?"

"I've plenty. I always have extra. I sell them sometimes, but we'll feed ourselves first and only sell what's left. Don't skimp."

"I'll eat four."

She nodded and turned, walking away.

Thankfully she was able to do most of the feeding using her left hand. Not that the palm of her right hand was burned, but she didn't want to risk scraping the blister and exposing the raw skin underneath. Not only would that hurt, but it would also be more likely to get infected.

She'd gotten the packet of bacon out of the freezer the night before to thaw. It was cooking in the oven when he came in the kitchen. When she heard his boots on the steps outside, she poured the eggs into the skillet which was hot and ready and pushed the bread down in the toaster.

She turned with the butter and a knife to set on the table.

He stood inside the door, watching her.

Suddenly the room felt small, and her lungs seemed to have a hard time expanding. And when she breathed out, her breath seemed to shake.

To cover her unexpected reaction, she said, "You can wash your hands at the sink."

She set the butter down on the table and didn't watch as he walked across the room. But when she grabbed the spatula to turn the eggs, she couldn't help but notice that he was holding his hands oddly and not allowing the water to wash over them like one would normally expect.

It made her look closer, and when his hand was just so, she could see the red and oozing blisters at the base of his fingers. She couldn't stop her gasp.

His head turned at the sound.

His cheek bunched, and he didn't say anything, but turned back to the sink and continued carefully running the water over his hands. He didn't use soap.

She wouldn't have either.

Maybe he was going to ignore it, but she wouldn't. "Your hands look worse than my burns do. I don't want you working on the fence anymore today."

"They're fine. The gloves help."

"Your hands will get infected, and then you'll be no good to anybody. They probably already are. Why didn't you say something?"

He snorted. She almost thought he wouldn't answer her, but he spoke, and his voice was a little sarcastic. "You grew up in Missouri, in Cowboy Crossing. You really think I would admit that my hands are sore and bleeding because I worked yesterday?"

Right. He was right. Of course he couldn't admit that.

"Well, you don't have to admit it. But we will both find something easier to do today. And tomorrow as well. And possibly the next day. After that, I think we'll be good."

"That's interesting. Yesterday, you were just telling me you have more work than you could handle, and it all needed to be done immediately. And now, we're just going to take the next three days off?" He blew out his nose and turned the water off. "I don't think so."

Well, that definitely raised her hackles. "Who's in charge here? Me or you?"

His jaw tightened as he reached for the dry rag and gently patted his hands. "I'm not going to be party to you being stupid."

She blinked, not expecting what felt like an attack. "I'm not going to take orders from someone who's supposed to be working for me. And who doesn't have a nickel in this."

He turned toward her, his perfect jaw square, obvious even under the stubble that gave him a rakish, rugged look. One that she definitely felt at the bottom of her diaphragm and that caused it to quiver, which she covered with a scowl.

His lips tilted in a smirk that didn't reach his eyes. "I guess me being bigger and stronger would be an advantage in this situation. You're not gonna do anything that's going to endanger your burns. And I'm going to build a fence."

Her jaw had to be jutting out just as far as his, and yeah, she might have to crane her neck way up to look at him, but that didn't mean she was going to take orders from someone who had no right to boss her around. "I will do whatever I darn well feel like doing, which will be what needs to be done. And you will do what I tell you to do." Her brow lifted. It was a challenge. "Or you won't be here."

He leaned closer too, bracing the hand that held the towel on the counter as his blue eyes speared into hers. "I'm pretty sure you tried to kick me off yesterday, and I'm here right now. So we'll see who wins. But I can tell you right now it's not going to be you."

"I'll call the cops and have you arrested."

"Are you going to ask to borrow my phone? Since you don't have one of your own?"

Okay. He had a point there. She had no phone. It was something that she had on her list of things to get, but it hadn't seemed necessary, since she never needed to call anyone. When she needed something, she just made a list and eventually made a trip into town, stopping to see the people she needed. Every once in a while, a phone would be nice when she had an order that could be phoned in. But making a trip to town had worked well for her, and she'd saved her money and not bought a phone.

Obviously, she regretted it now.

"I can drive into town."

"Everyone in town knows you bought me and that I'm supposed to be here for the next twenty-nine days." His face was so close his breath fanned across her cheeks. "You're not getting the police to remove me. They're holding a paper that says I'm supposed to be here."

"I'll tell them I changed my mind. That I want you gone."

His jaw muscles bunched in and out, and his eyes blinked, almost like he wanted to tell her something but was holding himself back.

Finally, he pulled back just a little, not conceding ground. "Maybe I want to be here. Maybe I feel I owe you. Maybe I learned some things about myself yesterday that I didn't like, and maybe I learned some things about you that I did."

If he took a squirt gun out of his back pocket and shot her in the face with it, she couldn't have been more surprised.

She touched her tongue to lips which were suddenly dry.

She couldn't even remember why she didn't want him here to begin with. Why were they fighting about this? It was like yesterday; their argument turned into something she didn't even understand and couldn't remember how it had begun or what had instigated it. Funny how she never had that problem in her life before, until Chandler.

"Your hands won't get better if you use them again today like you did yesterday." Her tone was softer too, although she wasn't going to budge on this point.

"I'm not. I'm wearing gloves. And I'm fine."

She'd hardly ever been around men. She'd lived with her mother and, for a while, her sister. Men had traipsed in and out the door, none staying long enough for her to read them or understand. But maybe there was some part of her, some feminine part, that recognized what seemed like a male need to prove himself. Or maybe it was just written on his face, although she didn't read that in so many words.

Still, she didn't want to set the precedent where he was the one in charge.

Even as she thought it, she wished for someone to share the burden with. It couldn't be a stranger though or, in Chandler's case, some man who was only here on a temporary basis.

Not for the first time, a thread of longing went through her. She wanted a partner. A friend. A husband and all that entailed. But she'd accepted long ago that would probably never be her life. Certainly not with Chandler. She hated that he made her feel things and long for things she couldn't have.

Still, apparently she wasn't strong enough to resist, because she said, "I guess you know your limits. The fence needs to be finished."

His head barely moved, but he nodded. She felt like they'd come to some kind of understanding, although she wasn't sure exactly what it was. Just that she'd allowed him to win.

Surprisingly, it didn't bother her like she thought it would. She almost felt relief.

Aware that they were still standing almost nose to nose, she realized he'd moved closer, and his eyes seemed to be searching hers. His breathing was just as shallow as hers, and the pulse in his neck ticked and jumped along with the sporadic beating of her own heart.

His eyes narrowed slightly, and his hand reached up.

She leaned forward.

Suddenly she realized the stench that she'd been breathing was the eggs, which she'd completely forgotten about, burning. She yanked her eyes away and jerked her body toward the skillet. The burned part of her hand bumped into his fingers as they reached out —she could only assume he was reaching for her—and sent sharp pain down her arm, balling at her elbow and exploding up her arm and back.

The big blister on the back of her hand popped from the friction, and the liquid in it seeped out, dripping off the bottom side as she grabbed the skillet and spatula and yanked it off the burner.

"Rats." There were other words she could say, words about the pain that was in her wrist, words she heard from the men who'd come to see her mother in the back room behind the various bars and restaurants all through her childhood, but she never said those words.

They represented the evil from when she was little. Somehow, she'd always known that she wanted to be different, and those were words that she couldn't say.

They didn't cross her lips now, but one or two of them tripped across her brain.

The bottom of the eggs was burned black, and the skillet smoked. It was her only one. Being that it was cast iron, she didn't want to put cold water in it, because it might crack, but she scraped the egg off, knowing it would continue to burn for a long time as the skillet would retain heat.

Chandler snapped the stove off and grabbed something from the table. He came back to the stove and cut off a pat of butter. It hit the skillet with its own hiss of smoke.

"That might help you."

"Thanks." It did help, but there was no way she was getting the rest of the egg off until the skillet cooled down enough for her to work with it. She set it on the cutting board.

"I'm sorry. I shouldn't have allowed myself to get distracted." Her frustration with herself was clear in her voice. "I don't have another skillet, but I can cook them in a pan."

"Let me see your hand." Chandler held his hand out. Her hand still burned, but she knew it would be okay. She'd scratched a small corner off, and all the liquid had drained out, but her hand was still mostly protected by the skin of the blister.

Still, she didn't argue with him but held it up. He took it in his, twisting it this way and that, before nodding.

"Now let me see yours." She couldn't help it. Her words came out as more of a challenge than a request. After all, she'd just trusted him to touch her hurt hand. She wanted to see if he would reciprocate.

Or if he was going to be the boss and not defer to her at all.

Something shifted inside of her when he held both his hands up in front of him, palms up, without hesitation.

They looked awful. And she really didn't have the slightest idea of what to do with them.

"Does it hurt to put soap on them?"

"I don't know. I didn't try. It just seemed like it would."

"I have some iodine. It might sting the parts that have been rubbed raw, but it will keep the infection away." She pursed her lips and tapped her toe, thinking. "I think we ought to wash them with soap and water and put iodine on them. I'll see if I can find some kind of ointment and a bandage."

"I'm not wearing a bandage." He glowered down at her.

She met his gaze but not in a combative way. She tried to give a little, because she kind of understood and knew where he was coming from or at least why. "I think you should. Your gloves will cover it."

They stared at each other; she felt swept away again in those same emotions, that compelling current, that she'd been in when the eggs had been burning. It was new, and a little scary, but she had to admit it was exciting too. She had a feeling, although she couldn't prove it, that she wouldn't feel this way with anyone but Chandler.

"You have stuff to make a bandage?"

"Yes. Just something to keep the ointment from rubbing off in your gloves. Then I think, but I'm not entirely sure, that you probably want to leave them open to the air tonight after you shower and are done working. It might help harden it."

He nodded.

It seemed like a good compromise to her. He would work on the fence, but he would wear a bandage like she'd asked.

He seemed satisfied with it too.

She took his hands and guided them to the sink, but she didn't put them under the water until she'd tested it so that it was still room temperature and not coming out too fast.

"You don't need to be all he-man on me. If this is too cold or too much water at once, just say so. I've never seen blisters this bad. I know they have to hurt."

"They do. But I've kinda gotten used to it."

"I don't think I believe that. There are painkillers in the bathroom medicine cabinet. They might help you get through the day too, if you insist on building the fence."

"I might take some when no one is watching."

Her eyes shifted to his. He looked at her with a little grin hovering around his mouth. She wasn't sure if he was thinking it, but she was definitely going back to yesterday when she was going to put her pants on but not while he was watching.

"It's a little different," she said.

"Not much." His lips parted even more, and his teeth poked out.

His smile grew hers. She shook her head and looked back at their hands. Her stomach had funny little flutters in it, and she had the oddest desire to stroke his hands instead of washing them.

"Okay. I think we've run water on them long enough. I'm going to put a little bit of soap on them. Just a little, and you can tell me if that burns."

"Okay."

She ran her fingers back and forth over the bar soap, lathering them up, before she took them and ran them carefully over his palm, just touching the edge of his blisters, careful to just do a little at a time, waiting to hear him tell her to stop.

His breath hitched, and her eyes flew to him. "Hurt?"

He shook his head.

She searched his face for just a moment before she went back. She had to believe him. But she didn't know what the caught breath meant.

Her heart thumped in her ears, and her fingers trembled as she rubbed more soap across his blisters, lightly and carefully.

Maybe it was his hand that trembled. Possibly from pain. His breathing changed, more harsh, and she was afraid she was hurting him.

Her hands stilled, and she turned her face, looking at his clenched jaw and his hooded eyes.

"Am I hurting you?"

"No." But his tone belied his words, sounding reedy and forced.

She turned back to his hand but didn't resume with the soap, unsure.

He pulled his hand away. "You're being too gentle," he said in that same tone that didn't fit with the words he spoke.

Confused, she looked at him, although she moved back and allowed him to have the sink to himself. "I'll go look for the ointment and the bandages. I believe they're in the bathroom."

He jerked his head but didn't say anything. She turned around and walked away.

Chapter Ten

Chandler stood at the sink, carefully scrubbing his hands. They did burn. That was true. But that wasn't the problem. Not in the slightest.

He hadn't expected to like Ivory. But he did. He hadn't expected to respect Ivory. But he did.

And he definitely hadn't been expecting to be attracted to Ivory.

But he was.

Never in his life had he thought that having a woman wash his hands could steal his breath, scramble his chest, and make him tremble.

Maybe he was just as disconcerted about that as he was about the woman who'd caused it.

He couldn't, wouldn't, be attracted to Ivory.

He could admire her, and he did. This was completely different.

He shut the water off and dried his hands, determined that this was not going to be a road that he traveled. He'd let her fix his hands, because he couldn't do it himself, and she was right about the ointment and the bandages and having them in the gloves. He needed them to heal and heal correctly.

That was all she was going to do, and whatever odd reaction he just had was not going to happen again.

He hung the towel up and sat down at the table as she brought things out of the bathroom.

Maybe she'd given herself the same pep talk, although nothing she'd done had indicated to him that she felt any attraction. She was too focused on her farm and working and being successful at whatever it was she was trying to be successful at here.

She obviously didn't have room in her life for a relationship or a man, and he wasn't interested.

They were a great pair. They had the same goals.

Her movements were brisk, and she had his hands covered in soothing ointment, bandaged, and finished in a short amount of time.

"You stay there; it won't take me long to finish breakfast. Just give me a few minutes to scrub the skillet. It should be cool enough to handle now."

It was on the tip of his tongue to tell her that he would scrub the skillet and she could cook the eggs. But he could hardly scrub with his hands the way they were.

Unless...

"Do you have rubber gloves?"

"I think there's a pair under the sink. Why?"

He stood. "If they'll fit me, I'll scrub the skillet. You can cook breakfast."

Her lips pressed together, but she didn't say anything. Walking to the sink, she bent over, reaching in and pulling out the gloves.

"They were big for me, which is why I never use them. I bet they'll fit you perfectly. Even with the bandages."

She was right; they did. And he took them. But he wasn't careful enough, and his fingers brushed hers.

Dumb. Because this time, he could feel the heat. It definitely wasn't something that either of them wanted.

She didn't see his other hand clench as he took the gloves and moved away from her, putting them on. He'd get through the next twenty-nine days, and so would she. But he wasn't going to touch her again.

———

IVORY WALKED up the hill to where Chandler was pounding the fence post. He'd taken the past week off from the heavy labor, helping her with the bee equipment and doing some light mechanical and other repair work.

They'd settled into a routine and rubbed along fairly well.

But this morning, he'd announced he was going to resume building the fence. She'd pressed her lips together, because while his hands had been looking better, they weren't ready for an entire day of abuse.

He'd been pounding all morning. Working steady, and as far as she could see, he hadn't taken a break.

She was a little early for lunch, but she figured his hands had to be in pretty bad shape. And if he'd taken any painkillers this morning, they'd surely worn off. Her burns were much better, but last week, she'd definitely needed a second dose of medicine at lunchtime.

She'd been able to do some things around the house, tending to her garden, cleaning some of the bee equipment and fixing what she'd brought down, as well as taking the clothes to the creek and washing them.

She always tried to wash her clothes pretty often, so she didn't have a big bunch to do all at one time. Eventually she was going to buy a washer at least, but she hadn't wanted to spend the money. There were too many other things she needed.

She knew she was kind of violating the unspoken agreement that she and Chandler had entered into. The one where he worked, wearing the gloves, and she left him alone, allowing him to do as much as he thought he was capable of.

If his hands were as bad as she suspected, she was angling to get him to take the afternoon off.

She carried their lunch in a bag, and she had a gallon jug of water from the spring and two cups in the other hand.

As always, her eyes wanted to linger on his shoulders and back. And as always, she was irritated at herself for being like the rest of the women in America. She kinda thought she was different, and it was discouraging to know that she wasn't.

Chandler glanced up as she came around his side, stopping a good five feet away. He jerked his head before he looked back and continued to pound the hole he was working on. His muscles strained against his T-shirt, and she found that fascinating.

Finally he slammed the digger into the ground and stopped, straightening, lifting his hat, and running the back of his gloved hand over his forehead before settling his hat back down.

The day felt pleasantly warm to her, but obviously with the labor that he was doing, he was hot.

She'd managed to have her wits about her enough to have a cup of water ready when he stopped. She held it out.

He winced as he pulled off a glove with his teeth. He only wore a small bandage. It was ragged, and she thought she saw bloodstains on it, but he kept his hand turned away, and she couldn't be sure.

"Thanks." He took the cup from her, careful to reach for the other side. As he'd done for the past week, he deliberately avoided touching her. Which was fine with her, except she wondered why.

Not that it mattered. Her goal was the same, so they were on the same page with that.

He drained the cup and handed it back.

"Another?"

He nodded. "Please."

She uncapped the gallon of water and poured him another glass, unsure why she was always so aware of his presence. Thankfully, her hands weren't shaking, although her heart wobbled some.

She handed it over again, and again he took it the same gingerly way. Then drained it.

She lifted the bag. "I have lunch. I thought we'd eat outside today, if that's okay with you. It's nice out."

He nodded, looking at his cup. "That's fine."

"I thought we'd go to the creek." She kept her face bland. She felt like she was deceiving him, but really, she wasn't. She just had a few more things that she wanted to happen, things she wasn't telling him about.

"That's fine. Sounds nice."

She turned to walk across the field on a diagonal to hit the creek at the spot she wanted, but his voice stopped her.

"I'll get that."

She stopped and turned, not sure what he meant. He dropped his gloves on the ground next to the post hole digger. Obviously, he thought he was coming back.

Not if she could help it.

He had his hand out, reaching for the jug of water and the bag she carried.

It was on the tip of her tongue to tell him no, she was fine, she wasn't helpless, and she could carry everything. Plus, his hands were hurt, while hers was healing just fine.

But she closed her mouth. There was something about the way he looked, or maybe it was the set of his shoulders, but she thought it was a pride thing.

She'd never really been around a lot of men who thought it was their duty to take care of women, but she'd read books to that effect. She assumed they were fairy tales. But Chandler looked like he'd be offended if she didn't hand over what he was asking for.

She gave a mental shrug. It wasn't going to hurt him to carry them, and he was doing it to be nice, not because he thought she couldn't.

She handed the bag over. "Thanks."

"Lead the way."

Maybe that was their compromise. He carried the bag, and she walked in front.

Probably she was just being fanciful, but she liked the idea that there was some give-and-take in their relationship. She didn't really want to be in charge all the time, although she needed to remember that this was her farm and he didn't care about it.

Still, the way he'd been working the last week, he'd certainly gotten a lot done.

The sky was blue, and spring flowers were bursting out all over the place, purple and yellow, and the smell of honeysuckle filled the air. She breathed deep and looked at the sky. It was perfect for what she wanted, with puffy white clouds floating lazily above them. A slight breeze blew, and off in the distance, one of her cows lowed.

She couldn't wait until she could get them in the pasture. They needed it. She had to be patient. So much of farming was patience.

She led them to the spot along the creek where it flattened out, rippled over rocks, and went over a little ledge where the trickle of the creek made a lovely music that was relaxing in any language or country.

Chapter Eleven

There was a nice grassy spot beside the creek tucked in like the crook of an elbow. Ivory took the blanket that she'd packed in her bag and spread it out.

"This is really pretty. I didn't even know it was here." Chandler sounded surprised as he stood and looked around.

"Yes. It's kind of hidden with that copse of trees there and the way you kind of go around the end of the hill. It's where I wash the clothes, and before I had a bathroom, it's where I bathed."

She dropped to her knees. He had been moving closer, but he stopped. "Before you had a bathroom?"

He said it like it was the craziest thing in the world for someone to not have a bathroom.

"It took everything I had to buy the farm. I didn't have money for updates."

He dropped to his knees, then twisted onto his rear, kicking a boot off. "I don't want to get your blanket dirty." He lined his boot up off the blanket. "I'm still trying to reconcile in my mind that there is someone in our day and age who doesn't have a washing machine and who bathed in the creek." He looked over his shoulder at her. "I don't want to offend you, but that's about the weirdest thing I've ever heard. I've never met anyone who lives like that."

She lifted her shoulder. Her goal had never been to be like everybody else. In fact, she'd spent a lot of time trying *not* to be like everyone else.

"I can't say you're wrong. It's weird."

He kicked his second boot off and twisted around, stretching his legs across the end of the blanket and acting as though he was going to lean back on his hands but remembered at the last minute they hurt.

"Let me see them, please?"

It wasn't a mystery as to what she was talking about, and he held his hands up to show her, but he didn't hold them out so she could touch them.

"I thought I saw bloodied bandages. We need to get them off. You should soak your hands in the creek for a little bit."

"You think that's safe?" His eyes narrowed as he looked at the clear, flowing water.

"Safe as anything else, I would say. It comes from a spring in the mountain, not too far from here. Water flowing over the ground purifies itself." He still didn't look convinced, and she couldn't offer him any guarantees, but she said, "I've drunk it plenty of times, if that eases your mind."

"Let me guess, you didn't have running water when you first moved in, either."

She grinned. He didn't seem like he was judging her or looking down on her. His mouth quirked a little. "You're right."

He shook his head. "I can't believe it."

"Maybe it would help if you didn't think about it." She had to admit she was teasing him a little bit. And she wasn't sure why. Maybe because it was just fun to share a smile. That was probably not all of it.

He looked out of the corner of his eye as he was taking off the bandage of his left hand. "I guess I can concentrate on the pain in my hands. That ought to take my mind off it."

"Okay. Go ahead. Think about how awful I am. And be scared."

He laughed outright at that. "I probably should be scared. If you're desperate enough to live like that, there's no telling what you'd do."

She hadn't thought about it as desperation, but she supposed, in hindsight, he was right. She was desperate. Desperate to be different. Desperate to have her own place, where she wasn't dependent on anyone, and desperate to get away from the people who looked down on her and made fun of her and tried to put her in the box that fit what they thought fit her, instead of letting her out to make her own life and reputation.

"You're kind of scaring me with that look. Anything bad?" he said calmly, like he asked people what they were thinking all time.

Ivory tried to think back. Had anyone ever asked her what she was thinking? She couldn't remember a time, but she hadn't had too many regular relationships. Even the one between her and her mom was definitely different. She supposed they got along okay, but Ivory deliberately didn't see her much.

"I was thinking that part of the reason that I did all of those crazy things was because I didn't want to be what everyone thought I was. I wanted to be something different. I guess I took different to the extreme."

"That's a good way to put it. Different to the extreme." The bandage on his hand unwrapped completely and fell off, exposing red, white, and pink flesh. Angry looking. And sore.

"Please don't try to tell me that doesn't hurt." She cringed at the sight.

"Even I can't lie like that," he said with a grin.

She didn't laugh at first, but then she remembered he was an actor. That must be what he meant. She chuckled.

"Here." She held her hand out, remembering too late about her earlier idea that he was avoiding touching her and that they were on the same page.

She just messed that up.

He lifted his other hand over without a word, and she took it, beginning to unwrap it.

"I wish I would have thought to bring a pan or basin or something that you can soak these in, although I really think that cool creek water will feel good on them."

"I'm not real concerned about that. As long as I can get whatever food you brought to my mouth, I'll be fine."

She laughed a little. "Okay. It sounds like we're eating first and soaking your hands second."

"That sounds like a plan to me."

She got the bread and the mayonnaise out and then pulled out the container of leftover roast beef from the night before, making him a sandwich.

She hesitated before handing it to him, wondering if she could ask him to say a blessing. She'd been praying over their food silently to herself, and he'd been letting her, respecting her decision with silence.

Thinking that it was probably just better for her to do it, she said, "I'm gonna pray."

She hadn't really meant to meet his eyes when she said it, but they skittered around and caught him watching her, and his eyes hooked hers.

They were slightly widened, and she had the feeling she'd surprised him, and he was contemplating the idea that again, she might not be what he thought she was.

She liked that, in a way. In another way, it made her nervous. She wasn't used to people seeing what she really was. And she used the baggy clothes, and the distance, and the self-sufficiency to keep herself hidden. Basically, they were walls. She hadn't even thought about it like that, but she knew right away it was true.

"I guess that means it'll be my turn at supper."

She forgot to breathe. Her words came out almost a whisper. "I guess."

Three slow heartbeats later, she tore her eyes away, bowing her head and saying a simple prayer, remembering to pray for his hands.

After she said amen, he looked up at her. "You forgot to pray for your burns."

"My injuries aren't nearly as bad as yours. They're healing up just fine."

"I see that." He nodded at her hand. He could see it while she'd been working on his probably. "It still looks sore. How's your leg?"

"It's fine. Better than my hand."

"I let you take the bandages off my hands. And I'll soak them after we eat. You can show me your leg."

"This is one of our compromises?"

His mouth tilted up, and her stomach flipped. "I think so."

So yeah, maybe he'd been noticing their give-and-take too. Maybe it had been a deliberate thing on his part, because she got the impression that he was used to doing things his way.

Of course, she was used to the same.

"Okay then. While you're soaking your hands in the creek, I'll show you my leg." Self-consciously, she tugged down her long-sleeved T-shirt.

It was a pleasant day, but there was just a little bit of a breeze, enough that she'd be chilly when the sun went behind a cloud.

Her long skirt wouldn't be a problem to lift up, but it did make her uncomfortable. She'd spent so much of her life trying to hide herself and not be like her mom.

Chandler looked at her, like he was trying to figure her out. But he could just go ahead and do that on his own, because she wasn't going to help him with it. It was hard enough to think about showing him her leg, even though he'd already seen it, and she knew it wasn't that big of a deal. Not to everyone else in the world.

It was a big deal to her. Because it was something that she hadn't done.

Deliberately.

She wasn't going to think about it right then though. She'd already agreed to show him. Later.

Using just one piece of bread, she made him another sandwich.

As she handed it over, she said, "I know you can probably eat about ten of these, but I thought it would be easier for you to eat with your hands the way they are if they weren't so big to grab a hold of. I'll make as many as you need."

"Make yourself one. I'm going to eat it all, and you'll not get any."

"Of course not. I'm going to eat. But you've been digging holes all morning, and I know you're starved."

"I haven't known you very long. At least, not long enough to know you know you." His lip quirked up, and she had to grin too. "But I'm guessing you didn't sit around and twiddle your thumbs all morning. Maybe you aren't doing what you might've been doing if you hadn't hurt yourself, am I wrong?"

She shook her head.

She made him another half sandwich before she made her own, and he was ready for it when she handed it over.

They ate a while in silence. The day was pleasant and beautiful, and the silence was sweet and enjoyable. A companionable silence. She savored it.

She didn't usually get to eat with people, and that was one time during the day that maybe she might have enjoyed some companionship.

He'd eaten four half sandwiches before he spoke. "So why are you doing all this?" It was almost like he could read her mind. "What's the point?" He waved the hand that held the fifth sandwich, indicating her farm and the work that she was doing.

She didn't know what to say. Nothing deep or private. "Doesn't everybody have to have a job? This is mine." It wasn't the answer he was looking for, but she hoped he would be satisfied with it. She didn't want to dig any deeper.

"I think you know that's not what I meant."

She lifted her brows, being deliberately obtuse. She'd probably tell him, if he asked directly. But she wasn't going to volunteer the information.

She didn't want to offend him by refusing though.

Even in high school, he wasn't shy, and he asked again, "Why did you choose this job? Why did you choose this?"

She took a breath in through her nose. He'd phrased it a little differently than what she was expecting, and she thought she could answer this one semi-safely.

"I grew up here in rural Missouri. Everyone farms. It was what I always wanted to do."

"When you say always, you mean it. You must've saved up for a long time in order to be able to afford this."

"That's part of the reason why it's so run-down. I had to buy what I could afford. But yeah, I saved for a long time."

His eyes narrowed, considering. "You were working before you were legally allowed."

"Legal work though." She said it almost offensively or defiantly. She didn't want him thinking that she had followed her mother into *that* profession.

"I hadn't doubted it."

She wasn't sure exactly if he meant that, but she appreciated the sentiment. She wanted to believe him.

"Are you ready to soak your hands?" she asked as she put the lid back on the mayonnaise and put it in the bag.

"Yeah. I didn't realize how much they were hurting until I stopped."

"It might be because of the bandage being taken off too. It probably will sting when you put them in the water."

"I was expecting that. Pretty much everything stings." He grunted, almost a laugh.

They moved to the creek, and he knelt beside it, leaning forward, gingerly putting his hands in the water, jerking them back one time before gritting his jaw and plunging them in.

It took about five seconds before he seemed to relax a little and more than that before the tension drained out of his shoulders.

Her hands had fisted in sympathetic compassion. "They must have gotten used to it. It looks like it's not hurting so bad anymore."

"You're right. The pain has dulled enough that I remembered you're supposed to be showing me your leg." He looked at her with a raised brow.

Her stomach did that crazy flip-flop thing again, although she still didn't want to lift her skirt enough to show him her leg.

But she also didn't want him to know how much she was struggling, so she gave her head a little toss and grabbed a hold of her skirt, bunching it so only the front of her leg showed.

His eyes studied the angry red dried blisters for a moment before they lifted to hers. "Better keep an eye on that. Looks a little red."

"I think that's natural. It's a burn after all, and it's dried up pretty nicely." She hoped it was. Her leg actually hurt less than her hand, so she figured it must be okay.

They didn't say anything for almost ten minutes while he kept his hands in the water. Finally he lifted them up.

"Do you think that was long enough?" He twisted them this way and that. They really did look a little better.

"Probably." She really had no idea. They might not even be doing something that was helpful. But at least they were doing something.

"It's crazy, but that actually made them feel better."

"It makes sense that it would. But I think we should let them dry out before we bandage them up again."

She stood. This was where she was hoping for a little bit of trickery. Hoping.

"Let's lie down on the blanket for a little bit." She moved away from the creek. "I like to look at the clouds. I always take a little time to do that when they look like they do today. What's the point of all this work, if you're not enjoying what God's given you?"

His brows twitched just a little, like he wasn't sure he believed her about watching the clouds. It was true. She did. But she did have an ulterior motive.

He nodded, and he followed her the few feet from the creek back to the blanket. She lay down on her back, well over on "her" side of the blanket, and he did the same.

She hadn't been around a lot of men for any length of time, but the ones that she'd seen would always fall asleep after a good meal if they lay down. She kinda figured Chandler might be the same with more than a few minutes' break. So yeah, she was being a little tricky, but it was for his own good. Because she was pretty sure he was going to insist that she bandage his hands back up and that he'd go right back to work.

She almost laughed and shook her head. Who would've thought that she would be trying to talk Chandler into not working so hard? She hardly thought that anyone in town would believe that. Maybe she didn't spend a lot of time there, but she knew his reputation.

"What are you smiling about?" he asked.

She turned her head toward his and looked across the three feet that separated them. She hadn't realized that he was looking at her.

She twisted her head back, looking at the clouds, and said the first thing that came to her mind. "Do you think that cloud looks like a gorilla?"

His head turned back up toward the clouds, but he grunted, almost like he didn't understand or didn't believe her.

But then he kind of chuckled. "Yeah. It actually does. You can see the arms hanging down the sides."

She smiled. "You sound surprised. You've never looked at the clouds before? Or did you think I made it up?"

"Both."

"You're kidding? You've never lain on the ground and looked at the clouds?"

"Nope. Admired the clouds in the sky. But I guess it just never occurred to me to lie down and look at them."

"Sometimes I like to bet myself on how long it'll take a cloud to roll across the sky. And I love to see how they change as they go. Something that looks like a gorilla now might look more like a house by the time it disappears into the horizon."

"I would never have guessed you for someone who wastes time looking at the clouds. I thought you are all about working all the time."

"No. Not all the time. Everybody has to take a break."

"The lady has changed her tune since last week."

"The man is being a little nicer to me than he was last week."

"Ouch." He shifted, but she didn't look at him. "Is it overkill if I apologize again?"

"No." She allowed herself a smirky little grin, thinking that maybe he wouldn't take it wrong when she looked at him. "You can apologize every day for the next twenty-three days, and it won't be overkill."

"I think your expectations are a little high."

"I think you can step up."

"You're the one that's mean to me." He held his hands up. "Look at my hands. That's mean."

"Oh, no, you don't! You can't blame that on me. You're the idiot that didn't stop. And I told you I didn't want you working today. You wouldn't listen. So no, no, and no."

"It was worth a try." His hands fell back to the blanket.

For the next fifteen or so minutes, they pointed at the clouds, talking about them some. And each time, the silence lasted longer and longer between them, until after about twenty minutes, he didn't say anything for a long time. Then she heard a faint snore and smiled to herself.

It worked.

Now what in the world was she going to do? She supposed she could lie on the blanket and look at the clouds. But she wasn't sleepy.

She had to congratulate herself on a good job, though.

Why had she cared? Why had it mattered whether or not he took a rest and took care of his hands?

She wanted to say it was just because she was a good person and didn't want to see him hurt any more than what he already was, especially since he was working for her. That was probably true.

But she also thought there might be a little bit more to the situation.

More about herself that she didn't want to face.

Chapter Twelve

The next morning, Chandler was still slightly shocked that Ivory had been able to so completely get him to stop digging the fence post holes.

He had to admit, as they left the house after breakfast, it actually made him feel pretty good. Almost like she cared about him.

Of course he wasn't entirely certain, because she wouldn't admit it, but he was pretty sure that she lay down on the blanket and made up that baloney about the clouds just to see if she could get him to fall asleep, and then when he'd woken up midafternoon, she'd said she needed help moving a bale in the barn before she fed.

He never had come back to the fence other than to get his tools and put them away for the night.

Now today, she was asking him to take a look at her tractor since she was going to be using it to bale hay soon. He suspected this was another ploy to keep him from using his hands on the fence, but again, he didn't ask.

"What did you say was wrong with it again?" Fixing machinery wasn't exactly his best area, although he'd done it growing up. What farmer hadn't? Something was always breaking down.

"I'm not sure exactly, but maybe you can just go over it and make sure everything is running correctly."

"It's always helpful to have an idea of what one is looking for when one is trying to fix something." She couldn't see his skeptical look, since she was walking in front of him, but surely she could hear it in his tone.

He followed her down the path, his eyes on her bulky sweatshirt and the gentle sway of her skirt around her ankles. Her leg must still be hurting her, since she was still wearing a skirt. She hadn't complained.

She walked with confidence, and he just couldn't bring himself to ask if this was her way of getting him out of using his hands. They did hurt.

As long as he kept his hands still, they were fine, but the idea of gripping the post hole digger and pounding it into the ground made his back muscles tighten painfully and twitch simply from anticipating how badly his hands were going to hurt.

Whether it was a ploy, or whether she really needed help with the tractor, he was going to go along with it.

They reached the barn, and she slid the door open, leaving it open, probably for the light, after they walked through.

"We could probably start with changing the oil. I have the filters and everything here. I was just kind of waiting for a rainy day to do it. But since you're already going to be looking at it, maybe you can do that, too."

"Yeah. That's not a problem. Good idea to start there."

Her tractor wasn't quite as old as he was, but it definitely wasn't new. He liked the fact that it didn't have a cab, and he smiled a little at the thought that he'd always thought that this was the way farming should be, closer to the air and dirt and less like sitting in a boardroom watching the seasons and the ground from the air-conditioned and cushioned seat.

The seat on this tractor was not cushioned.

She led him to a box behind the tractor. "Here's the filter, and I'd thrown the tools that I needed in the box. The oil is in there too."

He lifted the lid on the tractor and started working on getting the oil changed while keeping an eye on the rest of the tractor, looking for any wires that might be broken or for loose bolts. He hadn't been sure whether Ivory was going to stay or go, but she stayed at his elbow and handed him what he needed almost before he asked. He liked working with someone like that.

"So is this what you have planned for the rest of your life? Just happy here in your place, farming?" His question was kind of to fill the silence, since he'd always enjoyed socializing, but he was also curious about her.

She wasn't what he thought.

"I'm happy here. And I want to stay." She bent down and picked up the filter box, opening the lid. "I guess I don't have a life plan. If that's what you're asking." She seemed to be fiddling with the box, rather than taking the filter out, which was fine, since he wasn't ready for it anyway. "What about you? Are you going to be an actor for the rest of your life?"

"Yeah. It's the easiest money I've ever made. I just go have fun, for the most part, and they pay me for it." It wasn't quite that easy. Memorizing lines, working with difficult people, in difficult roles. But he really did enjoy his job and considered it grown-up playtime.

"All those people admiring you must be really hard to deal with too."

He could hear the sarcasm in her voice. "You know, you'd think you'd love to have people admiring you and screaming your name and just wanting a piece of you. But on one hand, it gets old. Seems like everybody wants you all the time, and you never have a break. And then on the other hand, it seems like no matter how often or how much or how many people say they love you and think you're wonderful, it's never enough. It never feels like you've arrived."

He could not believe he said that to her.

Lately he'd been noticing the contradictions, the ones where it felt like everybody wanted him and he never had a break, which was why he'd taken a month off to come back to Cowboy Crossing and probably part of the reason he volunteered to be sold at auction and agreed to one month's time. He just wanted to disconnect and be a regular person, not this idol that people made him out to be.

But at the same time, there never were enough admirers, the numbers were never big enough, there was always some insatiable part of him that wanted more admiration, more fans, more everything.

The box twisted in her hand, and a whole minute of silence ticked by, while he castigated himself for even opening his mouth. No one knew he felt like that. No one.

He felt exposed.

"I guess I'll have to take your word for it, since I've never had that problem. But I can kind of believe that, because that seems to be a hallmark of famous people—they always need more admiration, more money, more attention."

He hated that she'd lumped him into a group with everyone else. He felt like it was individually his problem, but he supposed she was right. It was probably the underlying problem behind people in Hollywood needing to be the perpetual fountain of youth—they'd do anything to stay young and continue to look beautiful.

"I'm not sure what to do about it. I can see it's been a problem for others, and I don't know how to keep it from being a problem for me."

"Probably being here is the best thing that you can do." She said that softly, and her hands had stilled.

She was right. That's exactly what he'd instinctively known—what had called him to Cowboy Crossing.

"I guess I know that on some level, although I've never articulated it to myself before. Coming back here grounds me. Nobody thinks I'm more than what I am, and there aren't those expectations to live up to. I don't need more adulation when I don't have any to begin with."

"Oh, I think you have plenty. I think you'll always have admiration just because of who you are..." She paused almost as though she wasn't sure whether she could say the rest, but then she did. "And because of what you look like."

He didn't understand how he was considered handsome. He didn't look that much different from his brothers when he looked at himself.

He hadn't meant to get into that though; he just wanted to talk to her and make conversation, so he tried to think of something that would lighten the mood. "Do I get all Sundays off?"

She'd given him the past Sunday off but hadn't said if it was a regular thing.

She snorted. "He's just been working a week, and he's more concerned about his day off than anything else."

"I have to say it's been a long time since I spent days at a time doing manual labor. It's not easy. Of course I'm looking forward to my day off."

"I still have the stock to feed and everything, but yeah, I usually don't do too much on Sunday. Maybe work with my bees."

"Isn't that scary? Dangerous?"

"What in life isn't dangerous?" She gave a little grunt. "Especially to a farmer."

"Good point." There were always so many things that could go wrong, so many different ways to have an accident, and who in a farming community didn't know someone who had been in an accident?

His phone rang out from where it was tucked in his back pocket. His agent knew where he was and knew not to bother him unless it was an emergency. None of his Hollywood friends, using the word "friends" loosely, had called him since he left town.

"You mind if I get this?" he asked, digging his phone out of his pocket.

It was probably someone in his family.

"Of course. You're not getting paid by the hour. I've already paid you. We'll just work a little extra tonight." Her words were light, and her expression, if not cheerful, was at least happy. She set the filter box down and walked away; he assumed to offer him privacy.

He glanced down at the vibrating phone in his hand, then wished immediately that he hadn't even considered answering it. It was his ex-wife.

"Yeah?" They hadn't exactly split on good terms, although both of them tried to pretend they had, and they also tried to be civil for the sake of their daughter, of whom his wife had custody.

She'd wanted it, and he hadn't fought her, not wanting to drag his dirty laundry out in the public eye any more than he had to.

"Good morning to you too, Chandler." There was just a hint of irritation in Jessica's voice. She really was a nice lady and a good mother. He supposed there had just been too much ego in their house for them both to get along. When he became more successful, she'd become more demanding, finally accusing him of cheating on her, which he hadn't, and leaving him.

There wasn't too much he could do about that. Protestations of innocence had been met with assurances of his guilt. She judged him guilty, with no evidence. She'd taken RaeAnne, their daughter, with her.

"Good morning, Jessica. It's awfully early, especially in Las Vegas." He did have a tendency to be a little gruff and forgo the niceties. He could try to be civil, even though he knew she wasn't coming back. In the two years since she left him, she'd lived with three guys—that he knew of—and she didn't seem to miss him at all.

He missed being married, and the companionship it provided, but he didn't miss Jessica. Too much ego in one house. That was what his agent said, and Chandler couldn't disagree. He wasn't an easy guy to live with either.

"Now that you mention it, it is early. You know I wouldn't be bothering you if it wasn't something of the utmost importance."

As he stood there, listening, he remembered he'd read a headline somewhere that said she and Bruce Swinger, her latest boyfriend, had split up. He never read the article but was pretty sure he'd seen it in the grocery store checkout line. Who knew whether it was true or not.

"What can I help you with?" He tried to infuse a little bit of friendliness in his voice, just for the sake of his daughter, but it was hard to imagine that he and Jessica had ever been more than passing acquaintances. He had no idea what they'd been thinking when they got married.

"I've been offered a movie role that I just can't turn down." She named an actress, one of the best in the business and one of the most sought after. "She's gotten sick on set and won't be able to film the movie. My agent told me that they want me to come and take her place. But it's on location in Africa, and I don't want to take RaeAnne with me. I want you to keep her."

Chandler didn't say anything for a minute, resting his hand on the exhaust of the tractor and staring down at the old barn's wood floor. What Jessica was saying didn't make sense, and he was trying to put the pieces together to figure out what she actually meant.

It was what he always had to do with Jessica. She never said what she meant. There was always an angle.

Finally, he just came right out and asked. "You and I both know there's no reason why RaeAnne couldn't be on location with you. You have a tutor and a nanny for her, and movie sets always have all the resources you need." He paused, to give his words weight. Then he asked, "What's up?"

Jessica sighed. He wasn't sure whether it was a put-out sigh or whether it was a sigh that indicated she was going to level with him. "You're right. I know you know all of that as well as I do. I didn't really want to tell you, but the set seems to be jinxed. There have been some freak accidents. You know how rumors swirl around this town. I just didn't want to take RaeAnne. I know it's perfectly safe, but I know that you're taking a month off, and you can have her anyway."

Jessica was right. He was taking a month off in Cowboy Crossing, then he had to be in L.A. to get ready for his next film.

There was just one small problem. He'd committed to working for Ivory for the next three weeks. He could hardly do that if he had his daughter with him. And he couldn't just bring her to town and drop her off at his mom's.

Still, he'd do whatever he needed to do for his daughter.

"You know I'll take her. Anytime. How are we getting her here?"

"The nanny will bring her. She was going to visit relatives in New York anyway."

He'd never met the nanny. She probably came highly recommended. Jessica was responsible and caring. But, the idea of his daughter on a flight across the country with a woman he didn't know didn't sit right. "No. I'll come out and get her."

He wasn't sure exactly how that was going to work, but he was pretty sure he could get Ivory to allow him to tack a couple of days onto the end, if he took a couple of days off to go get RaeAnne. Or if he needed to, he'd come back after his movie was filmed.

"Chandler, you don't have to do that. Larissa is perfectly responsible, and she can deliver RaeAnne wherever we need her. You can just pick her up at the airport."

"I'll be out."

The fact that Jessica didn't argue with him any more meant she was pretty desperate to get away, because he usually didn't win that easily.

They agreed he'd be going out tomorrow to get her and flying back the next day.

He let out a deep sigh as he swiped his phone off and let his hands rest on the tractor fender. He wasn't sure how this was going to work.

"Do you need a few minutes?" Ivory's voice startled him, and he looked up. He didn't know when she had left, but she was walking in the barn door. He hadn't even noticed she was gone.

"No. But I do need to talk to you. I know that things have been a little rough between us, but I need to ask for a favor."

"Yes?" She didn't seem like she was surprised or upset, and whatever anger she'd been harboring for him because of what he'd said all those years ago seemed to have ebbed, or at least she was hiding it better.

"I need to fly out to Las Vegas and pick up my daughter."

Her brows lifted, but she didn't say anything. She didn't look particularly shocked. It wasn't exactly a secret that he'd been married and had a child. His life was basically an open book with everything that he did announced through the news and regurgitated every time he had a movie come out.

"I need to go tomorrow, and I'll be back the next day."

She nodded, and her eyes dropped to his hands. "That might be good. Your hands could use a break."

"I know that's why you made up this baloney about the tractor, and all the other little odds and ends jobs that I've been doing, and that's why you had me sleeping yesterday on the pretense of looking at clouds."

She had the grace to grin guiltily. Yes, he'd thought so.

"I wasn't expecting this. I know I owe you another three weeks of work, or whatever, but I really need to take care of RaeAnne." He hated asking for favors, and his chest tightened while his feet fought to squirm.

"Your daughter comes first. And I appreciate you making sure of that. I certainly support it."

He hadn't realized her answer was something he was nervous about until his chest eased and his breathing evened out.

"Thank you." He looked at the tractor. "I can finish this today."

She nodded. "It's up to you."

He grabbed the filter wrench and picked up where he left off.

She came closer, and he said, "I know my mom can watch her

some, but I might have her with me. She's five and won't get in the way. Much."

"It's okay. Whatever we have to do to make it work, we will. And if it's too much, it's fine." She put a finger on the tractor fender and ran it along the smooth edge. "I...I bought you anyway, not really to help me, but because of my anger and bitterness at what you'd said. And after we talked, for this last week, I've been thinking, and I've realized how ridiculous it was I was still holding a grudge about something that you'd done years and years ago. It doesn't matter. And I need to let it go. So if you're here, that's great." She looked up, and her hand dropped back down to her side. "But if you're not, it's fine. Really. Taking care of your daughter is far more important anyway."

Her eyes held steady, and they stared at each other. He didn't know what he had expected. Since they'd talked last week, they kind of had a little bit of a truce maybe.

She'd managed to surprise him. Again.

"Thanks." His hands had stilled around the wrench, and he had the oddest desire to move closer to her. He shook it off, recalling all too clearly how tempting she seemed to be to him. And he wasn't sure why. She certainly shouldn't be.

"I'll assume you won't be here until I hear from you."

"It should only take me two days. After I get this oil changed, I'll look at flights. But I plan to fly out tomorrow. And get her the next day and bring her back. I know my mom will want to watch her, and she's the same age as Clark and Marlowe's children, so I imagine she'll spend some time with them. I don't know exactly how it will work out, but I appreciate you working with me."

"Sure."

She backed up some and stepped away from the tractor. He wanted to reach his hand up and stop her. He wanted her to come closer, not back away. But he didn't move. Just felt a little of the emptiness in the hollow beat of his heart.

"I have some other things to do. I'm going to go get started on them. When you're done here, and you have your ticket, if you still have some time and want to do something, please come see me. If we continue to take care of your hands, they'll heal faster. Two days away should really give you a good start on it."

He nodded, unsure what brought it on but noting that there was a bit of a change in her. More of a distance. He didn't like it.

Even if it was for the best.

Chapter Thirteen

Ivory was working in her garden in the late afternoon two days later when she noted a cloud of dust coming up the driveway. It could be anyone, but her heart beat a little faster, and she looked for the red color to come into sight that would say it was Chandler.

She didn't know why. They hadn't even spent that much time together, but when he left, everything seemed still and quiet, and for the first time in her life, she almost felt...lonely.

She just needed a glimpse of the crimson before she tucked her head back down and kept on weeding the onions. She grew almost everything she ate, with the exception of flour for bread and a few spices and other things, and her garden was a big part of that. She couldn't afford to neglect it.

What would Chandler's daughter be like?

Even at five, she would probably be beautiful.

With genes like her dad, and the beautiful woman whom he'd been married to, she would have to have perfect bone structure and features.

Not that Ivory cared.

Her own genes weren't exactly top-notch.

She almost snorted at that, but she'd gotten over it years ago. For the most part. Maybe she had a little chip on her shoulder. But there wasn't anything anyone could do about their genes.

She had left a note at the house to say where she was going to be, since she'd been expecting him to possibly show up today, although she hadn't talked to him since he'd left early in the morning the day after he talked to his ex.

He must have found her note, because barely five minutes after she'd seen his car, he came striding through the grass with a little girl skipping at his side, holding his hand and swinging it.

The girl's hair was in pigtails which curled down her shoulders. She looked happy, and it seemed like she was chattering. Chandler, of course, looked amazing as always and even better with the little girl beside him.

Her rebellious heart scattered and skipped and started to clap.

Ivory tried to concentrate on the weeds, but her lips wanted to curve up, and her whole body wanted to jump up and start walking down the hill to meet them.

She stayed where she was, head down, pulling weeds, until they arrived at the edge of the tilled patch of ground, and she looked up, hoping her face had at least a modicum of decorum still on it.

"Hi." Chandler's eyes landed on hers, and they didn't move. The little girl had stilled, too.

Ivory sat back, resting her hands on her knees.

She wore gloves today to protect her healing burn which was also wrapped. Normally she didn't use gloves in the garden, preferring to be able to feel the soil.

For some reason, she felt a little self-conscious with them on. Not that it mattered. She was being silly.

"Hi." Her eyes wanted to linger on Chandler, but she looked at the little girl. "Hey. You must be RaeAnne. I'm Ivory."

The little girl stared at her. Then it seemed like Chandler shook her hand a little, and the girl remembered she'd been instructed to speak. "I'm pleased to meet you, Miss Ivory. Daddy said maybe I could play here some and that maybe you would have some jobs for me to do too."

The little girl sounded older than five, almost like a little adult. Maybe that was because she had a lot of one-on-one time with her adult caregivers. Not that Ivory knew that much about children.

"Of course. I would love it if you would stay here and play. I always wanted to play in the creek when I was little. It's nice and warm, and the creek will feel good after we work some. Maybe you can help me in the kitchen a little too. Tomorrow I have to bake bread, and I could always use help with that."

The little girl's eyes had lit up, and Ivory wondered if she was used to being ignored. It almost seemed that way with the eager look that had crossed her face when she thought about working in the kitchen.

"Is that okay, Daddy?"

Chandler looked down at his little girl. Maybe it was just Ivory's imagination, but he seemed to look a little softer or not quite as rough with his hand holding hers.

"Of course it is, baby. As long as we don't bother Miss Ivory."

"I'm sure she won't be a bother." Maybe it was the little girl's curly hair that looked just like her sister's, but RaeAnne reminded her of her baby sister, in a way she hadn't thought of in years, and she almost wanted to stop weeding the onions and get up and go put her arms around her.

She shoved the thought aside, as well as the memories that wanted to well up in the back of her head. She had loved her sister so fiercely. It had been them against the world. And then God had taken her.

Ivory stood. "We didn't really talk about it, and I wasn't sure what you were thinking, but I assumed RaeAnne could sleep in the house with me."

Chandler nodded, looking off at the sun that was slowly sinking down over the hill. "I'm sure that would work for tonight. I think my mom will want to have her stay there some as well, and she can play with her cousins. Particularly for this weekend." He shifted on his feet and shoved his hands in his pockets.

Ivory's eyes narrowed just a little. She brushed off her hands. Chandler seemed to have more to say, but he was uncharacteristically stalling.

He cleared his throat. "My brother Deacon's always been pretty good at building things. It's warm enough now that we could add a little lean-to in the back of the house and put a bed there. It would only take a day or two to throw that up. Nothing fancy. I just didn't want to impose."

Ivory blinked. She hadn't been expecting this. Honestly, it'd only been about dinnertime today when she thought about trying to find a place for RaeAnne to stay. Probably because she'd been mooning over Chandler and hadn't been thinking of much else lately.

She had to admit his idea was better than hers.

But she said, "I couldn't ask you to do that."

"You didn't ask me. I offered."

"I couldn't allow you to do that." She didn't want to owe him in that big of a way.

"It would be you doing me a favor. Without that, we'd have my daughter sleeping in the barn, because I couldn't keep putting you out to have her in the house all the time."

"You wouldn't be putting me out. I offered."

They shared a smile, as her words echoed his. Still, she wracked her brain, trying to come up with a good reason for him not to do it. She didn't want him making such a drastic change on her property. The fact of the matter was she *would* owe him.

"Then you're okay with it?"

She shook her head slowly back and forth. "That's just too big of a thing for you to do. Normal people don't add on to someone's house. It's just not done. I can't accept that."

She didn't even know how to explain it. He was acting like it was no big deal. But it *was* a big deal.

A small gift, like a pair of gloves, maybe, wasn't a big deal. Adding a room onto her house? A completely different story.

"You said 'normal people.'" He spoke slowly and watched as his daughter walked around the garden, looking at the flowers and glancing down over the hill to the creek.

Ivory's eyes followed the little girl's gaze. When she was younger, and even now, it was a lot of fun to play in the water. RaeAnne would probably enjoy it.

The day was warm enough.

Chandler continued. "I'm not exactly normal. Not to rub it in or anything, but I am a kind of big-name movie star. Adding on to your house truly is no big deal for me." He kicked a stone with his foot, almost like he was embarrassed. But his eyes didn't leave hers.

She realized that was something that had shocked her over the week that they'd worked together. He wasn't arrogant and full of himself like she expected a Hollywood actor to be.

She had to admit she liked it, his small-town humbleness. She hadn't gotten that impression from him the night of the auction—he'd seemed cocky and full of himself then—but the more she was around him, the more she kind of thought that the way he'd been acting the night of the auction was the act and the way he was being right now was the real Chandler.

He blew out a breath. "Please. Let me make a room for my daughter."

She couldn't tell him no. She nodded her head. "Okay."

He waited a few beats, his eyes not moving, before he finally said, "That's it? No specifications on how it has to look, or where it has to be, or how big you want it? Just 'okay?'"

She nodded again. "I wasn't expecting a room to begin with. It's a gift. I'm not going to tell you how to do it."

"But it's your house."

True. "Pretty much anything that you do to it will be an improvement. We're agreed on that, correct?"

He laughed with her. "You said it. I think there's something rustically appealing about it."

"It's only appealing if you want to 'rough it.' Or if you can't afford anything else. It's definitely more appealing than living in town behind the restaurant putting up with what someone else wants every night in order to be able to keep my home."

Whoa. She hadn't meant to say all that. Although that's exactly how she felt. She'd rather live in a tent with no running water and cook over a campfire than be what her mother was. She didn't think that made her a bad person, but she supposed it did make her look like a fanatic.

Chandler nodded. He seemed to understand and not judge her. "If you don't mind, I've already talked to Deacon about it, and he said he can come out tonight and measure things off so we can figure out how much lumber we need and get started setting the footers on it first thing in the morning."

Her mouth popped open, and she put her hands on her hips. "You've already talked to Deacon about it? You assumed I was gonna say yes?"

He had a sheepish look on his face, and he lifted his hands up like he was somehow innocent. "That was just me thinking positively. I didn't know what you'd say. Although I really wasn't thinking that you might reject the offer to improve your house. I was hoping you wouldn't."

She shook her head. What more was there to say?

"Come on, RaeAnne, let's go down to the house so I can get a hold of Deacon and we can do some measuring before the sun sets and it gets too dark."

"Do I have to, Daddy? I want to go down and explore the creek." RaeAnne turned to her father but didn't start walking toward him.

"Not today, honey. It's not safe for you to be down there by yourself. And if I'm going to get a place for you to sleep, I need to get moving on it."

"But I don't want to go back to the house. I want to see the creek. Can't we walk down there first?"

Of course the little girl was used to getting her way. Ivory couldn't blame her. She'd much rather play in the creek than go stand around the house waiting for adults to get done with whatever work they were doing.

Ivory looked at the onion row. She had three quarters of it weeded.

"If RaeAnne can wait fifteen minutes, until I finish this row, I'll take her to the creek. I wanted to wash the dirt off myself anyway."

"You don't mind?" Chandler asked, low but serious.

"No. Not at all. I was going down there anyway."

He nodded. "Give Miss Ivory fifteen minutes to finish her work, RaeAnne. Then she'll take you down. But I want you listen to her." His voice was firm with an obvious command in it. Ivory wasn't sure that would get RaeAnne to obey, especially if she hadn't been taught that obedience was necessary, but RaeAnne nodded.

"Okay."

"If you want to, RaeAnne, I'll show you how to weed, and you can help me. We'll get done faster with two people working." Ivory didn't think the little girl would take her up on it, but she walked over.

Chandler's eyebrows went up too, like he was surprised as well. "Let me know if you need me to come get her or if she gets in your way."

"I will. But I think we'll be fine." Ivory smiled at the little girl as she stopped beside her. RaeAnne gave her a tentative smile back. "If you kneel down here, you can see the difference between the onions which have spiky things sticking up like this," she pointed to the onion tops, "versus the weeds which have kind of flat leaves." Her fingers touched the leaves of some weeds between the onions. "Can you see the difference?"

RaeAnne nodded solemnly. Ivory smiled. The little girl truly did seem interested, as some children were. Gardening wasn't for everyone, but from the time she could remember, she loved looking at the differences of plants and considering how they grew.

RaeAnne might not be as easily entertained as she was, but for now, it was new and interesting to her, and Ivory figured she could take advantage of it.

She taught RaeAnne to pull the weeds out carefully so she didn't pull the onions out with them, and RaeAnne did pretty well for a five-year-old, only pulling out three onions in the fifteen minutes that they worked.

By that time, Ivory was more than ready to go to the creek and rinse off. And RaeAnne was excited about wading in it.

It surprised her when RaeAnne took her hand as they walked down the hill toward the creek. Ivory looked down, and RaeAnne grinned up at her. Their hands swung between them, and Ivory started singing a catchy song about horses and ponies. Before they reached the creek, RaeAnne was singing some with her.

No matter how hot the day got, the creek was always cold, coming as it did from a spring up the side of the mountain. After they took their shoes and socks off and set them aside, RaeAnne squealed when she put her feet in and jumped right back out.

"If you can stand to keep your feet in it, you get used to it eventually, and it won't feel so cold." Ivory stepped in, bracing herself against the icy water. She hadn't exactly been planning on getting completely wet, but she'd worn shorts and a T-shirt, and she didn't see any reason why not.

"Is it very deep?" RaeAnne asked, a note of fear in her voice as she stuck her toes back in the creek.

"Nope. It doesn't even go to my waist. It definitely won't be over your head. I usually sit down in it when I want to take a bath."

"You take a bath in the creek?" RaeAnne asked incredulously, her big blue eyes wide, but there was also some intrigue on her face, like she was thinking she might not mind taking a bath in the creek.

"Before I had a bathtub and shower in my house, that's where I bathed all the time."

"I've never even been in a creek before." RaeAnne dipped her toes in again, squealing and jumping out before jumping right back in.

"I like to play in it and make little dams sometimes." She hadn't done it much, but that was what she would do if she had time to play.

RaeAnne tilted her head and inched a little further into the creek. "I think my feet are getting used to it now. They're not as cold."

"Sometimes it's just better to go in all at once as much as you can, rather than going little by little, because every step is a new blast of cold."

RaeAnne's perfect face and wide mouth scrunched as she considered what Ivory said before she inched a little further in.

It wasn't hard to see Chandler in the little girl. She had his nose, the shape of it if not the size, and his perfectly angled chin. Right down to the cleft in his chin. She had his blue eyes as well.

Just to prove a point, Ivory sat down in the creek. Her first instinct was to pop back up, because it was cold, shockingly so, but she forced herself to stay, and after a minute or two, she got used to it and the flowing water felt good around her. Meanwhile, RaeAnne inched in a little bit more.

Eventually she got completely wet and stopped just short of ducking her head under. Ivory didn't encourage her to do that, because that really would be cold, and they hadn't brought towels.

Still, when RaeAnne asked her to show her how to build a dam, Ivory got up and they worked on moving some rocks and stones and piling them in the creek.

Maybe an hour had slipped by, and it was getting pretty dark, but they were having so much fun and laughing together that Ivory hadn't even considered quitting. She probably should take time off and do stuff like this more often.

Chapter Fourteen

"**I** think we can start putting the footers in tomorrow." Deacon snapped the lid back on the can of fluorescent orange marker spray.

"Great. The sooner the better. I'd like to have RaeAnne here with me." Chandler could hear the occasional shout and splash from the creek. He wanted Deacon to leave so he could go see what was going on. Tinsley wasn't with Deacon, since she had been dropped off at their mother's. Otherwise Chandler would have sent her to the creek to play with RaeAnne and Ivory.

He had kind of expected them to be back at the house before he was finished.

"Hello?" Deacon said.

Chandler whipped his head around, embarrassed. His brother had been speaking, but he didn't have the slightest idea of what he'd said.

"Sorry. Spaced out."

"I saw that." Deacon tilted the can in his hand back and forth. "You and Ivory seem to be getting along pretty well."

"Huh?" Chandler blinked, trying to figure out if they'd been talking about Ivory and he'd missed it. "What makes you say that?" Had Deacon even seen them together?

"Mom said you two were in town together. Plus, you've been distracted all day. The kind of distracted that says your mind's with someone else."

"No." The denial was automatic. But Deacon's words rang true. He had been thinking about Ivory and wanting to go see her. Talk to her. Be with her. He'd been gone for two days, and it felt like years.

Deacon shrugged. "See ya tomorrow, bright and early."

"See ya."

Chandler didn't wait for Deacon's truck to leave.

He took off with long strides, more eager than he could admit to see Ivory. He didn't even really think he liked her that much, but he sure missed her when he was picking up RaeAnne in Nevada. He didn't even want to think about how much.

Deacon had hit the nail on the head.

As he went down the hill and rounded the bank, the splashing and laughing got louder, and he stopped for a second to watch.

It looked like they were building a dam, because they were lugging stones from the edge of the creek and dropping them in the middle. They'd gotten a bit of the foundation laid, although it didn't seem like they were aiming to completely stop the creek, just maybe having fun moving rocks and having the water come up a couple of inches.

No doubt his daughter was enjoying it. She was splashing around soaking wet, laughing, and dropping rocks.

He would've expected Ivory to be a bit more subdued, but she seemed like she was having just as much fun as RaeAnne, skipping and laughing and splashing.

RaeAnne had just asked her how many more rocks she thought they would need when Ivory, with a big rock in her hand, looked over at the dam. She didn't stop walking, though, and tripped, splashing down in the water.

Chandler took a step forward, worried that she might hurt herself, but she popped back up, shoving her hair out of her eyes and laughing. RaeAnne jumped over and splashed down beside her.

They laughed and splashed their hands in the creek, giggling and saying things he couldn't hear over the bubbling of the water.

He waited until they were both standing again before he walked closer to the creek. "I thought you guys would be back at the house long before this. That water has to be cold."

Ivory gasped, like she was surprised, and his voice had probably shocked her. But then she crossed her arms over her chest, like she was naked or something, and scrunched down, looking at him with wide eyes before plopping down completely in the water.

She was wearing her clothes and had undergarments on under them; it wasn't like he'd come upon her naked. But even as he was thinking that, he was remembering what she'd said about her mother, and he thought about how she'd probably lived with that stigma all her life and had done everything in her power to be the opposite of what everyone accused her of.

It struck him then that he was more of what she'd been accused of, and she was anything but.

He hadn't teased her or made fun of her since high school, but guilt still clogged up his throat. Maybe what she'd lived through then had made her what she was now, a woman of character that he admired and respected, but he didn't like his part in it.

"Daddy! Look what we're doing! Look at the dam we're building!" RaeAnne called out, unaware of Ivory's discomfort or his guilt.

He forced his lips to turn up. "I see that, baby. Looks good. What are you gonna do, make a pond?"

Her eyes got big. Maybe he shouldn't have given her that suggestion, because he could tell from the way the expressions rolled over her face she never thought of it.

"Do you think we could? That would be a lot of fun!"

He hadn't gotten to spend a lot of time with his daughter over the years. Not since he and Jessica had split. They'd face-timed and Skyped some, and he'd picked her up for the day. But he'd never seen her this animated or excited.

"Miss Ivory, do you think we could do that?" Her head swiveled back to Chandler. "Miss Ivory used to build dams all the time when she was little, when it rained and the water ran in the alley, and she and her sister would go out and play in the water. She knows all about making dams. And she's really good at it."

"Really?" Chandler said, but he wasn't really looking at his daughter or thinking of a reply, because somehow, it made him really sad to think of Ivory and her little sister that she loved so much and had been a mother to, because her own mother couldn't, outside in the back alley, playing in the dirty water that ran down the street.

But he didn't say any of that, and Ivory didn't look at him, still scrunched down in the water, only now her teeth were chattering. Her lips looked a little blue as well.

He figured RaeAnne wouldn't want to come with him, but he was going to make her, if only to give Ivory a chance to get out of the water and do whatever she felt she needed to do in order to be decent.

He averted his eyes.

"Come on, RaeAnne. We have everything laid out to start the room tomorrow with Uncle Deacon. Maybe he'll bring Tinsley with him and you two can play. Although not in the creek, unless somebody's watching you."

His eyes slid to Ivory just long enough to see her give a short nod. He moved them away, trying to respect her modesty. "Maybe Miss Ivory will have time after she gets some of her work done tomorrow. If not, I'll make sure you get a little bit of time once we get the cement in the ground and are waiting for it to harden."

RaeAnne's lips stuck out, but she turned and started walking out of the creek. It was crazy, but he actually had a wild thought of taking his shoes and socks off and wading in.

It had been years since he played in the creek. Although, it wasn't the idea of having fun in the creek that made him want to wade in. It just seemed like wherever Ivory was was where he wanted to be. That was a crazy thought, especially since she could barely stand him.

Funny that there were thousands of women in America who would love to be with him, but he couldn't get interested in any of those. Of course not. He had to pick the one woman who didn't want to have anything to do with him.

"We'll be up at the house." His eyes flicked over Ivory before he held his hand out for RaeAnne. She clasped it, and they started up toward the house.

————

Ivory took the last loaf of bread out of the oven and set it on the small counter. Golden brown and domed, it looked picture-perfect.

"I think you might have a knack for making bread, RaeAnne. These are the best loaves I've made in a long time." She smiled down at her little helper, who had turned out to be a pretty good right hand.

RaeAnne beamed. "They smell really good."

"I'm sure they taste good too."

"I just might have to test that theory."

Ivory's head jerked up. Chandler stood in the doorway, a tool belt around his waist and a cowboy hat on his head. She could see why millions of people flocked to see him in movies. He looked good. She could sit and watch him for two hours, even if the script and plot were awful.

"You're certainly welcome to have a slice, and Deacon can too if he's still here." Ivory closed the oven door and put the mitts in a drawer before turning to face him fully.

"He's already gone. And I'd love to try it, but I promised my mom I'd meet her in town because she's gonna take Rae and have a sleepover with her and Huck and Kylie. And then tomorrow night when they come back, we should have a room ready for her here."

He grinned at RaeAnne who grinned back and jumped up and down.

"I could take her. I needed to pick up the seed I ordered the last time I was in town so I'm ready to start planting tomorrow. It should be ready at the feed store."

She wasn't sure why she offered the way she did. Kind of like he wasn't welcome to come. Maybe she just couldn't find the words to see if he wanted to go too.

"That's fine... Do you mind if I tag along? I know RaeAnne has spent quite a bit of time with my mom over the years, but it's been a few months since she's seen her." He gave RaeAnne a reassuring smile and winked at her. "I just want to make sure that everything's okay before I leave her."

"I'll be fine, Daddy. I love Grandma, and we always have a good time when I go there."

RaeAnne wasn't shy; Ivory had already figured that out. And just like with being in the creek and with baking the bread, she was pretty open to new experiences and a joy to work with. Even if she was rather headstrong and insisted on her own way at times. What kid didn't?

"I certainly don't mind." She turned the oven off. "The bread is all out, and I'm ready to go. If we go now, we'll be back in time for me to make supper."

"I thought we'd just grab it at the diner." He sounded kind of hesitant and unsure. But it wasn't like he was asking her on a date. They were just conveniently going to eat at the diner since they would be in town at suppertime.

"Oh." She hadn't ever eaten at the diner.

Growing up, she'd lived behind the bars in town and the Mexican restaurant, and she'd had plenty of food from those places, but she'd never eaten in the dining rooms there. If she did get food, she'd taken it back to their apartment to eat.

Still, if RaeAnne could do all these new experiences, Ivory figured it wouldn't hurt her either.

"That sounds nice. Am I dressed okay?"

Chandler's lips curved up in that heart-stopping smile he had. Her stomach turned over, and she tried to pull her eyes away unsuccessfully. "Just like a girl to be concerned about what she's wearing. I'm sure you'll fit in. I'm wearing this." His hands indicated the dirty T-shirt and jeans he'd been wearing while they worked on the room. They matched hers. Although somehow it seemed more socially acceptable for a man to not be entirely cleaned up than it was for a woman.

But as long as Chandler wasn't embarrassed to be seen with her, she'd go the way she was.

"Okay. Let me grab my keys."

They left, closing the door behind them, and headed toward her pickup. They got in with RaeAnne in the middle, buckling her in her booster seat.

After Ivory had hers buckled, she pressed the clutch in and turned the key. All she heard were clicks.

Her stomach dropped, and her head started to throb. She wanted to lay her forehead on the steering wheel. "I think the battery's dead." She sighed. She had the battery charger, but she wasn't sure she had an extension cord long enough to plug it in and bring it over... It was going to take a while to figure things out.

"Let's go in my car. I'll get your truck started tomorrow morning, first thing. Okay?" Chandler unbuckled his belt and put his hand on the door latch.

"I couldn't ask you to do that. It will only take forty-five minutes or so to get things hooked up and get it charged enough so that it'll start."

She probably ought to get a new battery while she was in town.

Chandler looked at his phone. "If you don't mind, I'd really rather drive. I told Mom I'd meet her in an hour and fifteen minutes. We'll have enough time to eat supper together if we leave now. Otherwise we'll be late, and RaeAnne won't be able to eat with us."

She almost told him to go ahead and go by himself, but she didn't want to seem rude or snippy. He'd been so nice to her, and although it made her uncomfortable to accept the room, and now the ride, that wasn't an excuse to be mean.

"Do you mind putting the seed in the back of your car?"

"Not at all." His jaw was set, and she believed that he really didn't mind.

They got in his car, and he drove to town, answering a call from his mother on the way.

After he hung up, he said, "She's at the feed store now, and she said we could go ahead and drop RaeAnne off. I figured we would pick up your seed there too. We'll eat afterwards. She said she had supper in the crockpot for the kids."

Ivory didn't figure she could argue with his plans, although the idea of eating alone with Chandler made her nervous. As long as RaeAnne was there, it definitely wasn't a date. Being that it was at the diner, it still really wasn't a date, except she'd never eaten there. So it was kind of special for her.

Mrs. Hudson stood out on the sidewalk as they pulled up to the feed store. Chandler hugged his mom then said over his shoulder that he was going to help them carry out her seed. Which left Ivory standing on the sidewalk with RaeAnne and Mrs. Hudson.

RaeAnne immediately launched into a blow-by-blow of their time in the creek and making bread and how much fun she'd been having. Mrs. Hudson nodded, her eyes going to Ivory as she smiled and made appropriate noises to encourage RaeAnne to keep talking.

When there was finally a break in the action, Mrs. Hudson said, "It sounds like you've been having a really good time. I think Ivory must love children. It's been years since I've played in the creek. Ivory sounds like a lot of fun." Her crinkly blue eyes smiled at Ivory, and Ivory couldn't help but smile back. Mrs. Hudson had never been anything but kind to her and her mother. She couldn't help it if her son had been a jerk when he was a teenager.

He'd definitely grown out of it.

Mrs. Hudson's eyes shifted to Chandler as he came out hefting a fifty-pound bag of seed over his shoulder. She tapped her chin with her finger and looked at Ivory. "This coming Monday, we're having a Memorial Day celebration at our house. I would really love it if you would come with Chandler."

Ivory opened and closed her mouth. She needed to say no. She wanted to say no. But she couldn't get any words to come out of her throat.

"It's in the evening, so even if you do work, you just have to knock off a little early. We'll probably eat around six or seven, but people start coming around five. Everyone in Cowboy Crossing is always welcome. I'm sure you've seen the signs, but I've never gotten an opportunity to invite you specifically." Mrs. Hudson seemed to sense Ivory's reluctance. "It sounds to me that if you don't mind, you could bring some of your homemade rolls. They'd be really good."

"Oh, I couldn't possibly..."

"I think we should go," Chandler said. He'd come up beside her, and she hadn't even noticed; she'd been so focused on trying to figure out how to decline.

"You're certainly welcome to go. I would never make you work through that." Ivory hoped he'd take the hint and say he'd go without her.

"I couldn't leave without taking you. Please come. I think you'll really have a good time."

"Please do," Mrs. Hudson said. "I'd consider it an honor if you did."

"Please, Miss Ivory? I want my cousins to meet you!" RaeAnne's blue eyes pleaded with her from her sweet, little face.

Ivory could have said no easily to Chandler. She would have had a harder time saying no to Mrs. Hudson. But with RaeAnne chiming in as well, she was a lost cause.

"Okay. We'll plan on coming next Monday evening and bringing rolls. Is there anything else I can bring?" She'd never been to anything like this, but she was pretty sure that that was protocol. Bringing something.

"No one ever turns down desserts. So if you have a special one, you can make it." Mrs. Hudson's eyes twinkled, and she looked as pleased as any woman Ivory had ever seen that she'd agreed to go.

"She makes the best honey rolls, out of her own honey, and she had blueberries in them and cream cheese. I'm not even sure what they were, but they were really fantastic. Maybe I could talk her into bringing some of those," Chandler said, a little grin hovering around his mouth.

Of course he was relaxed; it was his mother and his home.

Ivory felt anything but relaxed. She didn't return his smile. Although her heart did warm to know that he had liked them. He'd said so at the time, but she didn't know if he was just saying it out of politeness. She kind of had to assume that, since he was suggesting she bring them now, he had truly liked them.

She nodded. "Okay. I'll plan on bringing that too, along with some rolls. You need butter?"

"She makes a really good honey butter to go with the rolls. I've had it on toast. It's pretty fantastic too." Chandler's offhand compliments were totally derailing her thoughts. She couldn't have protested now if she wanted to.

"Well then, it's settled. I'll see you on Monday evening if I don't see you before while we're shuffling RaeAnne around. Or maybe we'll see you in church on Sunday." With that, Mrs. Hudson gave a little wave, took RaeAnne's hand, and walked away.

"You don't look overly happy."

"I'm nervous. I've never been invited to anything like this before. I might end up doing something stupid and embarrassing you."

She hadn't meant to expose her insecurities, but Chandler just kind of looked down at her, his gaze dark and unreadable.

Finally, he said, "There's nothing stupid you could do that my family hasn't already done. And don't be nervous. I'll be with you. I won't let anything happen to you."

It wasn't exactly what she needed to hear to calm her nerves, but she knew he was doing the best he could.

She nodded, adjusting her wallet in her hand and walking into the store to pay for her seed.

Chapter Fifteen

Chandler sat across the booth from Ivory and looked at the steaming plates of food Amy had just set in front of them.

Ivory acted like she had never been in here before, had no idea what the menu that he had memorized said, and couldn't decide what to order. For a few minutes, he'd wondered if she could even read.

It was funny, but even if that were true, it hadn't changed anything for him. Maybe it just solidified the fact that he liked her more with every minute that he spent with her.

She was proud and industrious and nothing like what the town might have thought of her reputation, but she'd been quietly going about forging her own identity and her own place in the world, and she hadn't let anything stop her from doing what she felt was right. Not hardship, not lack of support, not lack of a social structure around her.

She'd been so sweet and kind to his daughter. Even though she had a ton of work to do, and would probably never get it all done, and certainly wouldn't get caught up, she'd taken the time to play with her in the creek and taught her to make bread.

RaeAnne couldn't stop talking about how much she loved and adored her.

Kind of like her father.

"Have you ever been in here before?" The question just slipped off his lips. The diner was kinda busy, and he saw some people he knew, including Wilder and his new bride who were neighbors to his parents' ranch. They raised expensive racehorses.

Wilder might originally be from North Dakota, but they sure grew them smart up there, because the guy knew his horseflesh.

"No." Her word was soft, her face pointed down at her food. She had a spoon in her hand, but she hadn't taken a bite. Maybe she was waiting for it to cool.

"Are you okay?" He kept his voice pitched low, although there was enough murmuring and talking that he didn't think anyone would overhear them.

"I'm just not used to being out this much and around so many people."

He nodded. He could see how being on the farm all the time would make her feel isolated and unused to social situations. Her experiences with those hadn't exactly been good either.

"Do you want to leave?"

Her head jerked up. "You haven't eaten yet."

"I don't need to if it's going to make you uncomfortable."

She shook her head. "Normal people do this all the time. I can do it."

"I think we already figured out that I'm not normal. I guess it kind of makes sense that you aren't either." He slid to the end of the booth.

Her eyes widened. "You're not really leaving?"

"It's more important to me that you're comfortable than I'm not hungry."

She glanced around the room, her eyes wide. "Sit down," she hissed.

He hadn't stood up, but he had been getting ready to. "Are you sure?"

She nodded. "Just eat fast." She grinned a little.

He slid in, grinning back at her. "Try your food. You might find it's good."

"Good will taste like sawdust right now. Maybe tomorrow I'll remember that it was more than edible."

"Actually, after tasting your cooking for the last week, I doubt anything they have in here will compare." He took a bite, chewed, and swallowed before he said, "Maybe you can sell some of your honey here. They might like it."

"It's a drive, but I can sell all the honey I produce in Springfield. Easily. I'm not really looking for new markets. Right now, I'd like to get more hives up. That's one of the biggest moneymakers on the farm, with some of the least amount of overhead."

"And you like it."

She nodded, surprise coloring her features, like she hadn't thought he'd notice. "I do."

"Maybe you get more money for it in the city, but I think it would be popular here too."

She nodded like she was considering it. Maybe she was. But he noticed that she avoided doing business in town if she could help it.

He wondered how much of that was because of the way she'd been treated when she was younger that had left the stigma in her mind about the way she'd be treated now.

He hadn't noticed anyone snubbing her or being unkind. Sometimes it was just hard to let those memories go. Like the way she'd held onto them with him.

Not that he was excusing himself, because he deserved her condemnation and wrath for what he'd done. And maybe these other people did too. But to think that they were doing it now... He didn't think that was true.

Maybe Ivory and he would never be anything more than almost friends, but possibly he could help her a little bit to find her place in the town or at least help her realize that the town didn't see her the way she thought they did.

"I'm glad you agreed to go to my mom's for Memorial Day. I would feel guilty going if you hadn't been going too, and I'd really like to see RaeAnne enjoy a holiday with my family."

"You're so good with her. How much time do you get to spend with her?" Her question was a little hesitant, almost like she was afraid she was prying. But he thought she meant it as a compliment. Because she just called him a good dad.

"Jessica has full custody. I didn't fight her on it. At that time, my career was just taking off, and an ugly custody battle would've been hard on everyone. I wanted to do what was best for RaeAnne."

"So you see her during the summers?"

He nodded. "Depends on shooting schedules. I can go visit her anytime I want. So when I'm not shooting film, I usually do. But Jessica and I can only spend so much time together before we want to kill each other."

He smiled a little at that, but Ivory's brows drew closer together. "Why?"

He set his jaw, his smile fading, and he sighed, looking at his plate. "I always kinda thought we both had an ego that was too big to get along with the other one. I have no idea how we stood each other long enough to get married. Just one of those infatuation things that wore off pretty quick, I guess."

"Couldn't you make yourselves get along?"

He shook his head. "She accused me of cheating on her, but when she left, she moved from my house directly into someone else's. Half the time, I wonder if she wasn't cheating on me, which is why she accused me of it."

Ivory nodded, her white blond hair moving on her shoulders. It looked as fine as spun silk, and he wondered what it would feel like.

He tore his eyes away and ate another bite of his meal.

She looked down at her plate and didn't say anything.

"What's the matter? I'm kind of getting the impression you feel like I should have tried harder or something. It's not like I didn't try."

"Sorry." She looked up, and although her eyes were sad, they also held no accusation or judgment. "I didn't mean to imply that at all. I just felt bad for RaeAnne, because I know what it's like to grow up without a father." She lifted her chin as though challenging him to talk about her father.

He'd never been one to back down from a challenge. "You had a dad."

"I did. He didn't live with us."

He felt bad immediately. "I had the ideal childhood. My parents loved each other, we grew up on a farm. I had a lot of freedom, although we were made to work hard too. But we worked hard, and we played hard. I was blessed." He looked at his fork, suspended in midair. "I'm sorry. I didn't mean to give you a hard time."

"I'm glad you see that." Her eyes were serious, and she looked into his, meeting his gaze. "If I ever have children, that's exactly how I would want them to grow up. Just like you did. With a mom and a dad, and plenty of space to run around, and plenty of work to keep them occupied and busy. I don't think there's any better way to raise children."

Before he could close his mouth, he grinned a little, and the words slipped out. "So you got the farm, you got yourself, now you're looking for the dad? Who's in the running?"

He thought he might have offended her or made her uncomfortable. For a minute, her brows did draw together.

But he supposed she deliberately decided to goof off with him, because she kinda tossed her head and a little grin tugged her lips up.

"You've seen how I live. I haven't found the guy who's willing to put up with all of that long enough to sweep me off my feet. I've got a feeling I'll be waiting awhile." Her words were light and teasing, but he kinda thought there might've been a certain sadness behind them, because who wanted to be alone?

He did. After dealing with Jessica, he'd decided that women and marriage weren't worth the aggravation. Although, maybe he was kinda changing his mind. Not sure if it was because he wanted Ivory, or because being with Ivory made him want what he didn't think he'd ever want again.

Whether that was with Ivory or someone else.

But even at that thought, he recoiled immediately. He didn't want someone else.

He swallowed, staring at the woman across from him. She was truly one of a kind, something fresh and unique and innocent when he wouldn't have thought there was such a thing left in the world.

"You deserve the very best that God has to offer you. I hope you get it." He used his napkin to wipe his mouth and put it on his plate, shoving it toward the end of the table. "Do you want dessert?" His tone was clipped, and he didn't try to modulate it.

"No."

"Then I'm going up and paying. As soon as you're done, we can leave."

He knew why he was suddenly in a hurry to leave and couldn't stand sitting there for one more minute.

They were way too different for there to ever be anything between them that could be worked out; he shouldn't even be thinking it. Or admiring her. But the idea of God having a man for her somewhere had irritated him to the point where he just couldn't sit still.

———

DEACON AND CHANDLER finished the room the next day.

RaeAnne, Chandler, and Ivory fell into some sort of routine, time-wise if not work-wise, for the next few days.

Ivory had to admit every morning she woke up nervous about the Memorial Day picnic. If she were being honest, she also had to admit that every day she woke up eager to work with Chandler.

She wouldn't have thought that she was the kind of person who needed other people around. In fact, she would have thought the exact opposite. But now that Chandler had been here, she was dreading his leaving.

He and RaeAnne made mealtimes more fun, and it was nice to have someone to talk to about the things that needed to be done, what priorities they should have, and how they could share the workload. He did a lot of the heavy work for her, and she knew when he left it was going to be hard to go back to the way she'd been.

Sunday morning, they went to church again, and there weren't as many smirks or behind-the-hand laughing as there had been the week before.

Chandler had assured her that it was because of her buying him and had nothing to do with her. But she wasn't so sure. All her life, people had laughed at her, it seemed. Nothing changed.

Except, she'd been going to church for a while, and people hadn't been laughing at her. She had to figure it was probably because Chandler was a big movie star and she was who she was. Seeing them together—such polar opposites—made people laugh.

All day Sunday, they took it easy, resting from their week of hard labor. They played in the creek and took a walk on the hill and talked about where she wanted to build her house someday far in the future when she'd saved enough money.

Sunday evening, they sat on the porch of her house and watched the sunset. RaeAnne had run around, catching a few butterflies that still flittered about as the sun went down.

She'd gotten tired and come over, and to Ivory's surprise, she'd settled down on Ivory's lap, cuddled up with her head tucked under Ivory's chin, with her feet curled up.

"Daddy, sing me a song like you used to."

Ivory blinked. She hadn't realized that Chandler sang. But then she vaguely remembered that he'd had a singing part in the school musical when they'd been in high school.

She knew her mouth was open, and he could probably see it, even though darkness was starting to fall. But she didn't want him to be self-conscious and was going to tell him so.

She should have known better than to be concerned, because he smiled, an easy, confident smile.

"Which one do you want, baby?"

RaeAnne moved and shifted deeper into Ivory's arms. "The one about the starlight and the moonlight, Daddy. Please."

"Sure thing, baby."

Ivory readjusted her arms around RaeAnne and couldn't stop the twirl of her heart as Chandler began to sing.

> *Beautiful dreamer, wake unto me,*
> *Starlight and dewdrops are awaiting thee;*
> *Sounds of the rude world, heard in the day;*
> *Led by the moonlight have all passed away!*
> *Beautiful dreamer, queen of my song,*
> *List while I woo thee with soft melody;*
> *Gone are the cares of life's busy throng,*
> *Beautiful dreamer, awake unto me!*
> *Beautiful dreamer, awake unto me!*

His voice trailed off as the song ended. Ivory kind of thought that RaeAnne might be asleep with the slow steadiness of her breathing as she rocked her gently back and forth.

But Chandler didn't ask; he simply started into another song. An old hymn, "Abide with Me," that Ivory vaguely remembered from her childhood.

He sang all four verses, and by the time he'd sung three more hymns, RaeAnne snored softly. Ivory herself was feeling sleepy, and her eyelids drooped.

Chandler stood, gracefully for such a large man, and moved closer on silent feet. "Here," he whispered. "Give her to me. I'll take her and put her down."

He lifted his daughter from Ivory's lap, leaning close, his breath blowing in her ear, moving the hair around her face. He smelled clean and fresh and like the strong, sturdy air of Missouri. It was a scent that reminded her of honest labor and close family. It started a longing in her heart to have that for herself.

He straightened, disappearing inside, and she stayed there for a few minutes, knowing that what she wanted was impossible and wishing that the longing that she had wasn't so strong.

Wishing too that he were leaving immediately. She wanted him to go before her complicated feelings got worse and she couldn't stand to watch him leave.

She heard his footsteps on the porch and realized she'd never stood up to go in herself. She stood and turned.

He was directly behind her.

She looked up.

"The last few weeks with you have been some of the best weeks of my adult life. Thank you for letting me come and for allowing me to bring my daughter here. I think this was about the best thing that could have happened to RaeAnne and me." His voice was soft, but she couldn't doubt the sincerity.

"I've benefited more than you have."

She wasn't exactly talking about the room that he'd added onto her house or all the things he'd done around the farm.

She was talking more about the bitterness that had faded away as she got to know him. About the joy she'd had in working with RaeAnne, and how he shared his daughter with her.

And yeah, even the feelings that he'd stirred inside her. Feelings she'd never dreamed were lying dormant in her chest.

"Ivory." His hand came up and touched her cheek. She hadn't seen it coming, but she didn't flinch away. Actually, she pressed her cheek into it and closed her eyes. It was rough, his blisters had healed and calluses had formed, and it scratched a little, but even that felt good.

"Ivory, I…I've been singing for RaeAnne, but the whole time I've been sitting there, I've…wanted to kiss you. If that's not something you want, you better say so now." His voice was just a thread on the late spring air, mixing with peepers down at the creek, and the hooting owl in the distance, and the far-off yapping of coyotes.

Those were familiar sounds.

But his words were foreign and new and terribly frightening.

She opened her eyes, her cheek still pressing in his palm, her heart beating crazily, and her breath almost coming in shallow gasps.

"No... No..." She swallowed. "I'm afraid." She couldn't believe she'd admitted that and didn't know what she was afraid of. Maybe of feeling more than she was ready to. Feeling more than she'd *ever* be ready to. Or of knowing that he would leave. Possibly knowing that it didn't mean anything to him other than a romantic liaison in the moonlight. And he'd had plenty of those, she was sure.

His lips pressed together, but he didn't move closer, and his hand dropped.

"I'm sorry." His gaze roamed over her face.

She shook her head, her eyes closing for a second. "No. I'm sorry." She blew out a breath. "I don't want to be something temporary for anyone. Not just you. I've never been interested in temporary."

He nodded, his expression closed. "I know. You're right. I can see that."

She swallowed and had to fight the urge to move closer to him. She wanted his heat and his arms, his touch and maybe even his kiss.

But she'd never been interested in temporary.

She was definitely interested in Chandler. Part of her wanted to take whatever she could get. She supposed that part was her heart. But her brain still had enough lucidity to remind her temporary, no matter how good, wasn't what she wanted.

Chandler wasn't long term. He would be good for tonight, she was sure of it, but she'd regret it, if not in the morning, when he took RaeAnne and walked away.

"Good night." He stepped back, then turned and took the porch steps two at a time, sauntering off into the darkness.

She watched him go. She had the willpower to tell him no—maybe it was self-preservation—but she didn't have the willpower to turn away, watching until he disappeared inside the barn.

Chapter Sixteen

Chandler was thankful for his daughter. If it hadn't been for RaeAnne, breakfast would've been awkward.

Stringing up barbwire wasn't the easiest thing in the world to do by himself, but thankfully Ivory had taken RaeAnne and gone to plant the corn seed she purchased.

It had been a really long time since a woman turned him down.

Actually, he couldn't remember it ever happening.

Ivory hadn't said she wasn't attracted or that she didn't want to kiss him. She'd said she didn't want to be a temporary thing.

She couldn't be the only woman in the world to think that way. He wasn't so jaded that he believed that. It was still an excuse he'd never heard before.

Part of him was embarrassed to have been turned down. But the bigger part of him admired her for sticking to what she believed in and wanted.

He could admire her and still feel awkward, because he hadn't been shy, and he'd told her exactly what he wanted.

To kiss her.

The lady had declined.

He still did.

Rejection stung.

It didn't matter how famous a person was, or how many people loved his movies or whatever, it still stung.

He didn't stop for lunch, figuring that if he worked straight through, he might have the fence finished. He'd been working on and off on it for several weeks, and Ivory really needed to get her cows in it. She was feeding them hay that she could use for feed next year, if she could just get her cows in this pasture. Not to mention, her cows would really enjoy all the green grass.

RaeAnne brought his lunch up—he figured Ivory would send something when he didn't go down—and he stood and chatted with her for ten minutes while he ate. She reminded him his mom was coming to pick her up at one so she could go and "help" get everything ready for the party. His mom was just looking for an excuse to spend time with her grandkids.

He knocked off around four, figuring that would give him enough time to get ready to go. He wasn't afraid to face Ivory, and he wasn't afraid to talk to her. It was just a little awkward after last night.

The sooner he faced her, the sooner it would fade.

He was looking forward to going to the Memorial Day picnic and spending time with her. She might not have any deeper feelings for him, but she was fun to be around, and they seemed to get along okay when he wasn't trying to push for more.

He'd take a friend. Although he'd like more.

By the time he got his tools, put them away, and got into the house, it was 4:30. Ivory was just coming out of the bathroom, wearing a long skirt that she'd worn when her leg had been burned, and to church each Sunday he'd been there, with a T-shirt that he'd seen before. Nothing fancy. He figured she probably didn't have any other clothes.

He was pretty sure she'd say she didn't have money to waste on clothes that she'd never wear. He'd like to see her in something nicer, because he knew she'd look good, but it truly didn't matter what she wore.

He jerked his head at the bathroom. "Are you done?"

She was holding a towel in her hand, and she fingered it, almost like she was nervous. Her blond hair hung in wet ropes down past her shoulders.

She nodded.

He walked closer to the bathroom, expecting Ivory to move, but she didn't.

"I'm...I'm sorry about last night." Her voice was so soft he could barely hear it.

He shrugged like it didn't mean anything and stopped right in front of her. Her knuckles whitened as she gripped the towel tighter. But she didn't back down.

"There's nothing to be sorry for. I asked. You said no. Happens all the time." His tone sounded a lot more casual than what he'd felt all day, and he was kind of proud of himself for being able to modulate it like that and pretend that her rejection hadn't stung.

She looked down and still didn't move. "I just, I just didn't want you to think that I didn't want that. Because I did. I kind of regretted everything after you walked away. I thought I should tell you."

All kinds of answers floated through his head. Chief among them was the desire to suggest that she could change her no into a yes right now. But he didn't want to do that to her.

She'd said no based on her values and principles, and after where he'd been, he had to admire and respect someone who even had values and principles, regardless if they went against his own desires and he ended up not getting what he wanted.

He shook his head with his lips pressed together. "Nope. I appreciate where you come from. And I respect what you're holding out for. I hope you get it."

Her throat worked, and she nodded slowly. "Thanks." She moved to the side, and he hesitated for a few seconds before he walked in the door.

They didn't say much on the ride there, but the closer they got, the more Ivory bunched her skirt up in her hands and stared out the window.

He made a comment about the weather, and one about the fence being done, and another about the work they had to do next week. She answered in monotones and syllables.

By the time they reached his parents' house, he was pretty sure she was contemplating grabbing the latch and jumping out.

Every year, his family sectioned off the lower pasture and threw the gate open wide so people could park in that field. It was just a short walk to the house and kept the driveway from being congested and from people being parked in.

He parked and shut the engine off, and then just sat there with his hands on the wheel. As he figured, Ivory didn't move either.

He suspected he knew what the problem was. It had everything to do with the inferiority complex she had where she thought everyone in town looked down on her. He'd sworn to fix it, but he hadn't done a very good job, and he didn't know what to do now, other than reassure her, but they were just words.

That's all he had. He opened his mouth. "I don't think you realize how much the people in town would like you if they knew you."

Her face jerked around, and her eyes were huge as she stared at him. "If they knew me? What are you talking about?" Her words came out fast and almost like an accusation, like the idea that he would suggest that they didn't know her was ludicrous. "I grew up in this town. Of course they know me."

"They know you to see you, but they don't know who you are, because you never talk to anyone." He could tell his words had had the opposite of his desired effect on her, because her eyes narrowed and her lips tightened.

"I thought you weren't judging me anymore. I should've known better."

He held his hands up. "I'm not judging you. Sorry if it came out that way. I'm just saying you're a really great person, and I know that everyone would love to have a chance to talk to you and get to know you."

"They've had plenty of chances."

He nodded, unable and unwilling to continue to argue.

How did he explain to her that she walked around with a chip on her shoulder, avoided town when she could, and only spoke when someone specifically asked her a question that she couldn't avoid answering?

Of course the townspeople didn't know that she wasn't what they thought she was. Of course it was wrong for them to judge her and to assume that she was like her mother, but part of the fault was hers, too, because she had never tried to show them that she wasn't what they thought. To show them she was different.

She was just angry that they didn't see it on their own.

"I'm sorry. You looked nervous, and I was trying to ease your mind. I guess I said the wrong thing." He hit his hand on the steering wheel and pulled the keys out of the ignition, ready to get out.

Her voice stopped him. "No. Don't apologize." She took a breath and let it out shakily. "You're right. I guess maybe in the back of my head I knew what you just said, but I never let myself think it."

He turned toward her, trying to meet her eyes, but she kept her eyes pointed down at her lap.

He spoke anyway. "I wish they could see what I see. What I've seen on your farm the last few weeks. You're a true Missourian. Hardworking, with unshakable values and integrity. You're funny, and you've been so sweet to my daughter. And you've been kind to me, even when I didn't deserve it. Give yourself a chance, everyone will love you."

She was still except for her fingers twisting in the material of her skirt, although not nearly as frantically as they had been.

"I guess you have to know I think pretty highly of you myself. If there's anything that I can do to make this easier for you, just let me know."

Two breaths later, and she looked up at him, meeting his gaze with a serious one of her own. "I misjudged you. And I'm sorry. Thank you so much for your faith in me and for your help."

They were talking about something completely different, but when she looked at him, all he wanted to do was lean closer and slide his hand behind her neck and kiss her like he hadn't been able to last night.

He shook those thoughts aside. That was obviously not what she needed. Not now. Not last night. Not from him.

"You ready to do this thing?"

His phrasing made her smile, and she laughed. "Yes. With you. Thank you."

They walked through the pasture toward the big front yard of his parents' place, carrying the regular rolls and honey rolls she'd made earlier.

He nodded and said hi to a few of his brothers but kept walking up to the table where the food was sitting. RaeAnne saw them and came running, throwing her arms around first him, then Ivory.

He could almost feel some of the tension draining out of Ivory as she hugged RaeAnne back and chatted with her for a few minutes. That was probably one of the best things that could have happened to her.

There was something about a child that could just make one feel loved and accepted. That's really probably what Ivory needed, not that he was a psychologist or anything. Far from it.

"Chandler! Ivory!" his mother said as she hurried around the table with her arms spread wide. "So glad you guys could make it!"

Chandler was a little taken aback when his mother went to Ivory first, giving her a huge hug and squeezing tightly.

Ivory met his eyes over her shoulder, and he grinned a little, shrugging. She grinned back before turning her head, closing her eyes, and squeezing, almost like she was just enjoying being enveloped in a hug. Made his heart clench a little, to think about the upbringing that he'd taken for granted and left without too much thought. It was something that she hadn't had and cherished.

Ivory and his mom chatted for a bit before his mom hugged him, and his dad came over and shook his hand.

Marlowe joined his mom and Ivory's conversation before she put her arm around Ivory and said, "We have time before we eat for a game of badminton. If you guys wouldn't mind, Clark and I need some people to play against who are taller than four feet." Marlowe hit Chandler's arm as she walked by him. "Come on, boy, Clark's going to want to whup your butt in badminton." Out of the side of her mouth, she said to Ivory, "Sorry about the trash talk. It's a family thing."

"You don't have to apologize, and it's probably going be true. I haven't ever played badminton. Is it hard to learn?"

Chandler took three long strides and caught up with them, walking on the other side of Ivory.

Marlowe removed her hand from Ivory's back so she could gesture as she explained to Ivory that badminton wasn't any harder than using a racket and hitting an object over the net and back.

He was a little concerned that Ivory might be feeling overwhelmed, and he put his arm around her, intending to lean down and whisper in her ear.

Her face twisted toward his, and he couldn't mistake the relief in her eyes as she leaned into him a little. Maybe she just needed that human contact from someone familiar. He didn't know, but he kept his arm around her, putting his mouth next to her ear.

"Are you okay with this?"

She nodded, then lifted her head, so he tilted his. "As long as you're with me."

"I'm not leaving you."

The woman lived by herself and supported herself on her farm, taking care of all of her animals, dealing with weather and any problems that arose. She wasn't timid, and she wasn't afraid. Not normally.

It made him feel good that he could give her his strength now. Maybe help her a little. Which was odd for him, because most of the time when he was with a woman, he'd been looking to see what was in it for him.

He hadn't realized until just now, but his relationship with Ivory was different. Definitely more of a give than take.

He liked that she made him a better person.

But he didn't want to analyze it too much, so he just allowed her body to curve into his and enjoyed the feel of the warm woman beside him, knowing that for now at least, they were a team.

A team that got beaten pretty bad at badminton.

Ivory hadn't been joking when she said she'd never played before, and he was pretty rusty as well. He hadn't played badminton since before he left for Hollywood the first time—that was obvious by how poorly he played.

It didn't take long for Clark and Marlowe to beat them. It wasn't a shutout, but it was close.

Still, Ivory was laughing by the time they were finished, and he was pretty sure she was enjoying herself, feeling much more comfortable now and having made a friend of Marlowe.

By the time they finished up, RaeAnne stood with Huck and Kylie, Marlowe and Clark's children, and Tinsley alongside the court area.

The children happily took their rackets, and the adults walked off the makeshift court which was basically just a net put up in the middle of the yard with two two-by-fours marking the back of each side and invisible lines stretching out from the sides of the net.

A lot more people mingled about, and it was nearly time to eat. Marlowe still talked a mile a minute to Ivory as they turned and began walking toward the tables.

Ivory glanced back at him, and he fell into step beside her. He allowed his hand to brush hers once, then twice.

She didn't move away, and so he slid his hand around and threaded their fingers together. She allowed it, folding her fingers over his, not exactly clenching tight but holding on.

He squeezed her hand, and she squeezed back.

He knew what his family would probably think, looking at their joined hands, if they hadn't already suspected something when he walked down with his arm around her. But it was making her feel better, and he'd just have to explain to everyone later that it didn't mean anything. Although he was pretty sure he'd never brought a woman home and walked around holding her hand. Even Jessica had only been back to Missouri with him once or twice, eschewing what she considered country life.

He pushed that thought aside and enjoyed the feeling of walking with someone beside him. Almost like he had a partner. It wasn't a bad feeling.

Actually, it was the kind of feeling he enjoyed. He knew there was no competition between Ivory and him like there had been with Jessica.

He wasn't blaming that on Jessica. It was as much his fault as hers. The competition.

The divorce, on the other hand, he had to blame on her, if there was going to be blame cast. He had been pretty involved in his career, but so had she.

Regardless, it was nice to walk beside someone that he knew was going to support him, and would encourage him, and wasn't out to one-up him. That was definitely not Ivory. Even when she didn't like him, she wasn't trying to put him down.

Chapter Seventeen

The evening went by quickly, and he thought they had a
good time.

He did.

Ivory seemed to as well.

His oldest brother, Reid, who had four kids of his own, got the
tractor and wagon out and was giving hayrides by the time it got dark.

RaeAnne had never been on a hayride, and after the first two
times, he'd been unable to get her off the wagon. Not that he tried
that hard.

A few people had left, and after he'd waved to RaeAnne once
more, he leaned over and said to Ivory, "You want to take a walk?"

She seemed like she'd done pretty well all evening, talking with
people and laughing. He thought she enjoyed herself. He enjoyed
watching her. It was kind of fun to be with someone who wasn't
concerned about their appearance or his. And who wasn't bored out
of their mind because the people that they were with weren't quite on
their level.

He thought that maybe Ivory would be ready to step away for
little bit, and RaeAnne obviously wasn't ready to leave.

Okay. Those were all excuses. He just wanted to be alone with Ivory for a little bit. He wanted to savor the feeling of walking beside her and holding her hand.

Maybe just wanted to talk to her for a bit.

She looked up at him, smiling. The anxiety and insecurity that had been on her face when they arrived was completely gone. He'd like to think he had something to do that, but he was pretty sure it was just because of the kindness and downright goodness of the people in Cowboy Crossing, and because of Ivory's own personality and her tendency to be able to correct herself when she saw that she was wrong.

She smiled and nodded. "I'd like that."

He wasn't sure exactly how they looked, but when he raised his head from speaking low with Ivory, his eyes happened to meet his mother's. She was watching them.

She and Deacon were standing together, Deacon with his hands crossed over his chest and his legs braced. Alone.

When Deacon saw him looking, one side of his mouth curved up, and he nodded his head almost imperceptibly.

Chandler jerked his in return, although he wasn't sure why. If Deacon was trying to say something, he was missing the memo.

He tugged on Ivory's hand and started across the side of the yard toward the barn. He figured he probably didn't have too many women that he'd ever been with who would appreciate a tour of their barn. But he knew without asking that Ivory would.

They walked in silence until the lights and laughter of the party faded away.

"Thanks so much for staying beside me all night. I know that made it a little harder on you, and you didn't have as much fun as you could have, but I appreciated it."

"It didn't make it harder for me. It made it more fun." He supposed he could have elaborated, but he'd already stepped out of line the night before when he asked to kiss her and she shut him down. So he kept his mouth shut and lifted his head to the breeze which felt warm and soft, carrying with it the smell of cut hay which sweetened it and made him breathe deeply. "I love that smell."

"Me too. It doesn't make me hungry, but it makes me want to go roll in it or something." He could hear the laughter in her voice, and he had to agree.

"It's not hard though to figure out why cows love it. Man, there's just something good about that smell."

They walked along in silence for a few steps before she spoke. "I think I met all of your brothers tonight. There are four, right?"

"Five. Including me, it makes six boys for my parents."

"Oh, okay. That's right, I guess I did meet six. Reid, who has four children?"

"Yeah. His wife left him while the youngest was still bottle-fed. She was a liar and a cheat." He shouldn't have said that. But she was.

"Hmm." It was probably smart of Ivory not to comment. He knew he was biased, because he loved his brother.

"And of course I know Deacon, because he was close to our age, and Clark." She hesitated for a minute. "Maybe I'm prying, and just tell me if I am, but Deacon was never married, was he?"

"No. He's the only one that wasn't."

"What's the story on Tinsley?"

"I have no idea. Deacon won't say. She just arrived one day—a newborn in a car seat dropped off at the church—with a note that said Deacon was her father. He didn't deny it, so we assumed the note was correct and he knew what was going on. Deacon was the least of us who might have had something like that happen to him. We'd never seen him with a girl anyway." He kind of laughed. "If we were Catholic, he'd be a priest."

"Yeah, I remember he had that kind of reputation."

"He's been a great dad. Totally devoted to being a dad. Tinsley's been blessed. Even though, as far as I know, she doesn't know who her mom is either."

They'd reached the driveway, and he walked back down it,

leading her toward the dark shadow in the distance. "I kinda thought you'd like to see our barn."

"I bet that's the first time you've ever said that to a girl." Her voice held a teasing note and a light one that he enjoyed. It took him back to the days over the past few weeks that they'd worked together in easy silence or companionable talking.

"You'd win that bet." He could laugh. And he did. "I think I like hanging around girls that I can say that to."

"Girls?" Her voice was still light and still had the teasing note, but there was a vulnerability there that he hadn't noticed before.

"Just you. You know there's only one of you."

He meant it as a compliment, and he thought she took it that way when she laughed.

"We milked our cows here, although we lived where Clark still does. Mom and dad didn't build that fancy new house until a few years ago.

"Hmm."

He wasn't sure what that meant. The way he grew up was a lot different than the way she did. Maybe that was what she was thinking.

They reached the barn, coming to the milk house first. "This is where the tank used to be. Back when we milked cows. We sold them when I was still in elementary school. There's just no money in milk, and the market is too volatile. It's been taken over by the factory farms."

"Yes," she said. "I've seen that, and I think it's sad. Although I do think that organic and pasture-raised milk could be sustainable for a small family farm. A lot of work though."

He nodded, again realizing that she wasn't like the girls he normally hung out with. He'd forgotten. He didn't need to explain to her about agriculture or the death of the family farm. "You're right. It would be a lot of work, it *is* a lot of work, but there's definitely a demand for that. I'm thinking it'll grow, too. If I were getting into farming, that might be a good niche to look at."

"If you had ten kids to help you with the work."

He laughed. "Ten kids *is* work in itself. I can't imagine that."

"You have a pretty close example of it growing up with five brothers. And from what Marlowe said tonight, she made the sixth sibling."

He nodded slowly. "Yeah. I guess my mom made it look easy. But you're right, six isn't that far off from ten."

"I feel bad for your mom though. With all those boys, she didn't have much help."

"Oh buddy, she had help. We didn't have a choice about working in the house or working outside. There was always work." That was part of the reason he left the farm. Too much work. Work that didn't feel like farmwork when he was sitting in his air-conditioned, GPS-driven cab. Not the kind of work that a farmer would do.

Ivory grunted. "I guess she didn't have a choice. If she did try to do everything for you guys, she would have died from work overload."

"Yeah. And before we sold our cows, she was out working in the barn too. I can say that about my mom, she sure knows how to work. And my dad. Not to dismiss him, but we were talking about Mom."

"You and your dad look an awful lot alike. You have the same mannerisms too."

"I hope someday I'm half as good a man as he is. I know I'm not."

"He's got some years on you. Give yourself some time."

He grunted but didn't answer. "And here's the parlor. I guess back before my time, they had a stable. And again before my time, they replaced it with this double eight. They sold some of the equipment when they sold the cows, but I think in the back of his mind, my dad always hoped to milk again. He loved it."

"You know, I think there's just something about cows. You always hear about people loving horses, and there are tons of books and everything written about that, but there's just something about cows that gets in your blood. It's hard to shake them."

He laughed, but he thought she was serious. He could see from the way she treated her own animals that she truly did care about them. "So cows are your favorite animal?"

"Yes. They are. I'm telling you, there's just something about them."

"They even beat out kittens?"

She laughed along with him. "They sure do. I'll take a cow any day over a kitten."

"Man. I've worked with you for several weeks now, and I had no idea how weird you were."

"I'm scaring you, aren't I?"

"Yeah. You are."

"Then I guess I better not give you my opinion on anteaters."

He snorted. "If we're going to remain friends, we better not talk about anteaters. I can see that won't end well."

They laughed together again, and he was feeling light and happy. It was pretty much the way he always felt when he was with Ivory.

Her fingers moved in his hand, and he turned toward her. Her face was serious as she looked up at him.

"I feel like it's only fair, after last night, that I tell you, while I really like you and I feel like maybe we are friends, what I feel for you is not friendly."

He blinked. Her words had been so hesitant and soft it took him a little bit to figure out what she was actually saying.

"I guess you already know I feel that way. I don't typically go around asking to kiss my friends."

She nodded, her lips ghosting a smile. "I assumed you didn't."

He needed to be as honest as she. "But I've already done the long-term thing. It didn't work. And now I only get to see my daughter occasionally through the year. She leaves and doesn't live close." He resisted the urge to pace. "That's the hardest thing I've ever had happen to me, when my wife left and took RaeAnne with her, and there wasn't anything I could do about it. I can't do that again. Marriage just doesn't seem to work for the Hudson boys."

There was bitterness in his last line, and he hated that, but he didn't know what to do about it. Because it was true. All of them had tried it. All of them had failed. Except Deacon, who'd ended up with a kid but no marriage.

She nodded. "I appreciate you being honest with me. And I appreciate you respecting my decision."

"Of course. You have just as much right to your decisions as I have to mine."

Her fingers jerked in his. "Do I have the right to change my mind?"

His mouth dropped open, and he stared at her, trying to figure out if she meant what he thought she meant.

He thought she did.

"Yes." This word was a whisper.

"Good. Because I have."

Suddenly he felt like he was breathing like he'd run up a steep hill, and his heart pounded just as hard. But he didn't want to make inferences. He needed the straight truth.

"You changed your mind about kissing me?"

Her brows twitched, and she lifted her shoulder. He wasn't expecting to see the little turning of her lips that indicated a small smile. "I changed my mind about you kissing me. I'm not sure how I feel about me kissing you. I hadn't really thought about that."

"Maybe we can talk about it."

"Is that how you usually do it? You talk about it?"

His own lips twitched, and although his heart and lungs still weren't working together in any kind of comfortable rhythm, he could appreciate the humor. "No. It's not. But I'm also not usually laughing when I'm getting ready to kiss someone for the first time."

He didn't want to talk about all the other first kisses he'd had. It seemed like it wasn't the thing to do when he was getting ready to have another first kiss. Hopefully.

"I've been telling myself over and over for the last few weeks how you're so much different than any other girl I've ever met. It figures you'd be different with this too. I want to kiss you, and I want to laugh, and here I am talking about it. I guess I don't have to tell you this isn't my first kiss, but it's definitely my first kiss like this."

Humor flashed in her eyes, and he was pretty sure, far from offending her, his words had made her happy.

"Maybe we can quit talking now?"

"I've quit for a while. But I don't mind listening to you either."

"I don't think this is something I can talk about while I'm doing it."

"I guess you'll have to show me then." Her brow lifted in the challenge.

He'd never been one to walk away from a challenge. He tugged on their joined hands, and she stepped forward. She was close enough to kiss, but not close enough to satisfy him. His arms slid around the curve of her waist, harder than he had anticipated, but he supposed that made sense since she spent most of her days in constant physical labor.

"Why are you smiling?" he asked into her upturned face. It wasn't a nervous smile. Actually it was a smile that made *him* nervous. If a woman could look at a man with stars in her eyes, that's how Ivory was looking at him.

"When I got dressed tonight, I thought you might be ashamed of me. I don't look like everyone else. Plus I'm weird in a lot of other ways."

He started to disagree with her, but she shook her head, a finger coming up and touching his lips. There was no pressure, but he liked the way it felt.

He touched it with his tongue.

Her eyes widened, and her finger dropped.

"You're not weird."

"I am. But you acted like you didn't mind being with me, no matter what I looked like or how I acted or even what my reputation is."

"It wasn't an act," he said honestly. "And it's not that I don't mind, I liked being with you. Loved being beside you." His hand came up and cupped her cheek. It was as soft as it was last night, only tonight, he didn't think she was going to tell him no. "I feel like we complement each other. Like when you're beside me, it's not about who can draw the most eyes, or who can be better than the other, it's like it is when we work together—we help each other."

If possible, her smile softened even more. That look made his heart beat hard, but his stomach cramped and curled. He wasn't sure he could live up to that look, wasn't sure he wanted to face what he thought it meant.

Ivory was strong and tough, but for all that her mother had been, Ivory was naive about relationships. She wasn't holding anything back, and everything she felt was right there on her face for him to see.

He didn't deserve that trust. He definitely didn't deserve what he thought he saw there. Admiration, respect, and—possibly—love.

It all scared him. She thought he was more than what he was, gave him more credit than he deserved. He could bluster along—he was good at that—but in his heart, he knew, had figured out over the last few weeks of working with her, that he wasn't good enough for her.

She was real—solid and strong and exactly what she was.

While he was a fake. Just pretending to be the person whoever he was with thought he was.

Except when he was with Ivory. She brought out the man he wanted to become.

Not now, though. The man he wanted to become wouldn't kiss her when he knew she was looking for something permanent and he had no plans to stay. No plans to enter into any relationship that would last beyond a few kisses.

He should back away, but he leaned closer, pulling her toward him until their bodies touched.

She made him better. Maybe he could be better in this, too.

"You told me no last night." He managed to get the words out, his lips almost brushing hers.

"I'm sorry."

"Don't be. I just want to make sure you truly changed your mind."

"Yes." She stretched up and brushed her lips against his.

He closed his eyes, his hands tightening around her and his breath hitching.

She did it again, and he had the same unexpected reaction. He should have known. Nothing with Ivory had been the same as it had with anyone else.

She stretched up once more, and this time, he met her halfway, allowing their lips to brush before he parted his and deepened the kiss, pressing her to him, pushing his hand into her hair, and vaguely realizing it felt as soft as it looked.

Her body moved sweetly under his hands, pressing closer. Heat pushed through his chest and down his arms as her hands slid up and around his neck, a light touch that burned deliciously and made him tremble.

The old milking parlor wasn't the most romantic spot in the world, and maybe he should have picked a better spot for their first kiss, but he wasn't thinking of that, didn't have any coherent thoughts other than he needed her closer and didn't want to ever let her go.

———

Ivory padded out of her house and walked around the back. She couldn't keep from smiling and for some reason, her fingers wanted to linger on her lips which still seemed to tingle.

From not wanting to go to the Memorial Day picnic at all to having the best experience of her life there, it had been an enchantingly wild evening and she couldn't sleep.

But she wasn't out to have a midnight tryst, either, so she didn't walk down to the creek, which would take her right by where the object of her thoughts was sleeping.

She tucked her arms around her waist as a cool breeze floated across the dark night, but she didn't really feel it.

Chandler was the most amazing, wonderful man. She'd enjoyed their time together as they'd worked on the farm, but tonight was beyond anything she'd imagined. Not just the kiss, although that had been beautiful beyond words, but the way he'd treated her and the way she'd felt when she was with him.

It was easy to see she'd fallen in love with the man.

The thought stirred her heart and made her dreamy smile grow bigger.

But, it was also easy to see that he wasn't the permanent thing she'd always wanted, that he wasn't viewing them as a long-term item, and that, even if he felt a fraction of what she did, he wasn't going to be staying.

He had a career, a *very* good one, in Hollywood, as well as legions of fans, and he'd be going back to it all.

Soon.

Those thoughts were enough to sober her some, but not enough to dampen the tender feelings cocooning her heart.

After he left there would probably be pain, she realized that, although she'd never had her heart broken before. Maybe she was being stupid, like millions of women before her down through time had been for men who would never commit and who would just leave – her mother, for example – but Ivory had a new perspective on those women, now.

She could understand the pull to spend whatever time she was granted, falling deeper and deeper in love with a man, who might love her back, but would never stay.

She sighed.

Her defenses hadn't been strong enough and it was too late to build more now.

Her choices were either to enjoy the time she had left, and worry about the heartbreak when he was gone, or push him away now, hoping to ease the eventual pain and separation.

The inclination of her mind was the second – the less pain, the better. But her heart wanted to enjoy whatever time she could have with him, and honestly, it seemed harmless enough. It wasn't like she was planning on having an intimate relationship with him. Just sharing smiles, holding hands and more sweet kisses.

She had to admit, though, one kiss only made her want more.

The risk was worth it, she finally concluded, still smiling her dreamy smile, and pushing back hard on that little voice that told her she was allowing her heart to rule her head and that's where a woman's troubles always began.

———

CHANDLER HELD Ivory's hand as they moseyed in from the pasture where her cows and goats now grazed with contentment.

They'd gotten the fence up and he'd spread fertilizer for her. Her beehives were all fixed and ready, plus he'd made some improvements in the barn.

Her corn was just poking through the ground.

They'd had a busy and productive week.

It had been the best week of his life. He'd never had so much fun with another person.

And, at night, after RaeAnne had gone to bed, Ivory and he had strolled hand and hand under the stars, kissing and talking and cuddling. It had been the perfect ending to each day of hard labor.

He'd savored every minute.

But today was his last day here.

His mother had wanted to spend one last afternoon and night with RaeAnne, leaving him to have one last afternoon and evening with Ivory. He hadn't been able to figure out how to say what was in his heart.

What he was feeling was so unusual and different from anything that he had ever felt before.

Or ever wanted. He was treading on completely new ground and he wasn't sure how to handle it.

He knew exactly what he wanted – Ivory – but he wasn't sure how to get her. He wasn't even sure if Ivory wanted him.

But tonight was his last night. He was leaving first thing in the morning. He had to figure out how he could make Ivory his. Let her know that was what he wanted.

His thumb stroked her hand as they walked along, her body lightly brushing his and her scent drifting up. They seemed to always head towards the creek. The sounds and gurgle of the stream and the scent of moist earth and honeysuckle mixed together in the night air.

For the rest of his life, any of those sounds or smells would bring him back to the beauty of this week and the gift of time that he been given with this woman.

She didn't say anything, and he waited until they reached the edge of the bank, where they stopped. He tugged on her hand until she turned and they faced each other.

With easy familiarity, she stepped into his arms, and he closed them around her. He didn't bend his head to kiss her like he had every other night they'd done this. Instead, he pulled her close and put his hands on her back, lightly touching.

"I wanted to talk to you for a minute tonight."

Her shoulder shook like maybe she was laughing. "You can talk to me if you want. But I wanted to kiss you for a minute tonight."

He laughed. If he thought back to that first day when she'd taken him home from the auction, he never thought that they would end up where they were, wrapped in each other's arms and standing by the creek together.

"This wasn't how I pictured us thirty days from the day you bought me." He had to share that thought with her.

"It wasn't exactly what I was thinking was going to happen either," she said with a smile in her voice.

"Life has a way of surprising us sometimes, doesn't it?"

She nodded. "It sure does."

"Well, it surprised me in a couple of other ways too." He took a shaky breath, unable to remember when he'd last been this nervous, but determined he was going to say something, anything, to try to keep her with him. Or keep them together. Or...what exactly did he want?

"We haven't really talked about what happens after I'm done shooting this next movie." That wasn't too bad of a beginning line.

Ivory didn't say anything, but she tensed a little under his hands.

He opened his mouth again. "I was hoping that between films you and I can spend some time together. I mean, I like kissing you, and I'd like to be more than what we are right now. I would like..." His voice trailed off. He didn't even know how to articulate what he wanted to say. Was he asking for a long-term relationship? Would they be a couple?

Ivory didn't move, but it seemed like there was a distance between them that hadn't been there before, as she tensed even more.

He didn't want to scare her away, and he didn't want to take things too fast. It had only been a month. He wanted everything from her, but feeling her pull away, made him think he needed to back off.

"I mean, I'm not saying we need to be exclusive or anything." That was what he wanted. But maybe a full-blown relationship was too fast for her. Maybe he was doing this Hollywood speed, rather than Missouri farm girl speed.

The one thing he did know - she hadn't wanted a relationship with him to begin with because he told her he tried the marriage thing and hadn't worked out.

But, if not marriage, then what?

His phone rang in his pocket. He ignored it, letting it go to voicemail. This conversation was too important to interrupt.

"Maybe I'm being selfish." His hand ran down her back and over her shoulder, curving around her neck under the soft curtain of her hair. "Maybe I'm asking you to be with me and you aren't ready."

Her breathing had gotten more shallow, but he didn't know what that meant. Had he upset her?

He waited for long minutes. His phone rang, and he let it go again. He wanted to know, needed to find out from Ivory, what was between them.

Finally, he said, "Talk to me, Ivory. Tell me what you're thinking."

"It might be best if we just break it off. It was a nice little fling for a month, but there's no future. You coming back will just drag it out."

He swayed, his fingers tightening before he forced them to relax.

Maybe it shouldn't have, but the effect that her words had on him surprised him. He hadn't expected to feel it that deeply.

Was this how she really felt? Before he could collect his thoughts and talk to her, his phone rang again.

"I think you better answer that," she said softly pulling back some, until there were was an arm length between them, and just his fingertips rested on her shoulder.

He tried to look down into her eyes, but the night was too dark. Or maybe it was his mood. Gloom seemed to settle over him, heavy, cold and hurting.

He reached into his pocket and pulled out his phone, swiping without even looking to see who it was, not wanting to take his eyes off of Ivory.

"Hudson," he answered.

"Chandler, did you see the news?" It was his agent, Randy Bieler.

"No. I haven't watched the news in a month." He hadn't missed it. Too many other things had captured his attention.

"Where are you? On safari in Africa?" Bieler asked. But then he said, "Never mind. Jessica is dead. Killed on the set. You'd better get your butt to Las Vegas, they're sending the body back, and you are definitely going to need to be there."

Ice flashed through Chandler's body and his head spun. Jessica was dead? His stomach tightened in a sick knot.

"Chandler?" Randy's voice prompted.

The last thing he wanted was to go. Jessica was his ex - he wasn't married to her. But everything in show business was all about show. He knew that. He had been there long enough and he understood. To not show, to not have his daughter there, would look bad. Really bad.

Jessica might not have been quite as big of a name as he was, but she still had a pretty large following, and he needed to play the game.

But...his daughter just lost her mother. How was he going to handle that? How was he going to tell her?

She would be devastated.

How does one tell a daughter their mother died? He backed completely away from Ivory and blew out a breath, running his hand through his hair and tilting forward slightly. Agonized at the thought of how his daughter was going to feel. What he was going to have to do to her.

He always wanted to protect her, keep her safe, make her happy. Provide for her. This was not one of the things he wanted to have to do. Far from it.

"Chandler? Are you still there?" Randy's voice came over the phone.

"Yeah. I'm just trying to figure out what I'm going to say to RaeAnne."

"Don't tell her now. I'll get Dr. Will on the phone. He'll fly out to Vegas, and he'll help you figure out the best way to break the news to her. You just need to be there."

"How much time do we have?"

"Her body arrives tomorrow. There's going to be a big hoopla."

He didn't have any time. He'd have to leave right now, and hope there was a red eye he could catch.

Man, he hadn't processed the thought that his ex-wife had died. He wasn't in love with her anymore, of course, but still, she'd been so alive. So beautiful and vibrant. It was hard to believe that life was snuffed out.

"They're closing that set down. There have been accidents and whispers that it was cursed, and now with this fatality, there's no way they're going to finish that movie over there. They'll probably build a set here in Hollywood or on location somewhere in the states."

"Yeah." Chandler didn't know what else to say, his mind was roiling with so many other things.

His eyes shot to Ivory. He couldn't see her in the dark very well, but he thought she still faced him. She was probably wondering what was going on.

He wanted to lean on her and share this with her. Sharing the pain halved it right? He wasn't sure, but he'd be willing to find out. Ivory made them better in every way. It made sense that she'd do so in this as well.

But he couldn't. He couldn't do that. It wasn't fair. She had just said she thought it would be better to have a clean break.

New pain, fresh pain, harder pain, hit him then. She didn't want him.

She had basically...broken up with him.

His lungs choked, and he couldn't get his chest to move out.

He could handle Jessica's death. He could do what needed to be done. RaeAnne would be the worst, and that was going to be hard. Just as hard as reconciling the fact that he was losing Ivory, had already lost her. She wanted a clean break.

"You still there buddy? I didn't think this was going upset you like this. I'm sorry. I should have broken it a little bit easier to you."

"No. I'm fine. I need to get RaeAnne, book a flight, and I'll be in Vegas in the morning."

"I'll get your flight. You just get to the airport. Call me when you're on the way, and I'll text you the details of the flight."

"Okay."

They hung up. Chandler stood, just breathing. Trying to process.

"Is everything okay?" Ivory asked softly. He couldn't mistake the caring in her voice. She might want a clean break, but she still cared for him.

Maybe he wouldn't have said the words if he hadn't been shaken by both Ivory's breakup and Jessica's death. "I love you. That was what I was trying to say earlier. I love you. I wasn't expecting to, didn't want to, but I do. And I know I said I didn't want to get married, that I'd already had one failed marriage and didn't want to do that again. But that's what you deserve. Marriage. And that's what I wanted." He raked a hand over his hair.

She started to speak, but he put his hand up. "No. Please. That was my agent. Jessica died on the set. They're shipping her body back and I need to be in Las Vegas with RaeAnne tomorrow morning." All the words seem to come out a rush, all the wrong words. He didn't want talk about his ex-wife in Vegas and funerals and sadness. He wanted to try to figure out how to convince Ivory to give them a chance. "I want to kiss you before I go."

He shouldn't have asked, but he craved her touch and scent and taste and needed to take as much as he could with him.

"Okay." Her word was soft and whispered and immediate.

He was grateful for small mercies. He felt like he needed her now more than he ever had before. Needed her kiss, needed that closeness, and he was afraid he would have been on his knees begging if she hadn't said yes. He didn't wait, because he kissed her hard and deep. He meant to be fast, but ended up not.

He lifted his head, sucking in air. "I need to go." His hand found hers in the darkness. "I'll walk you back."

"No." Her hand squeezed, but then slipped out of his. He felt the loss just as sharply as any other loss this evening. "I want to stay here for a while."

He wanted to have more time with her. As much as he could get. Just the walk back would be a few more minutes that he would cherish and didn't want to give up. But he couldn't force her.

"Okay." He had so much he wanted to say, that he wanted to talk about. He should've done this earlier. But he wanted to finish out the time he'd committed to before stepping forward into something new. He'd needed time to think. Plus, he hadn't known what was going to happen tonight.

"I don't know what's going to go on with the funeral and with everything that's involved in that. Then I have to start that movie, and I'm going to need to be on location. It'll probably take a month." Wait. Why was he telling her all of this? She said she wanted a clean break.

It was the last thing he wanted.

He swallowed around what felt like a lump of sawdust in his throat. He wasn't going to force her. He couldn't. He needed to walk away with dignity and respect her decision.

"Take care, Ivory. Knowing you has made me a better man."

Chandler turned and walked off into the darkness, before he couldn't.

———

Two months later.

Ivory turned off the small flatscreen TV and plunked down on the bed that she still thought of as RaeAnne's.

It had been a rough two months, and she'd lost even her desire to work and save to build a farm that she dreamed of.

She'd taken some money out of her savings, bought a TV and had watched every movie that Chandler Hudson had ever made.

She was so pathetic.

But it had been necessary. He wasn't the marrying kind, she'd known it, and all he was offering was for her to be his booty call between movies. "Kissing and more" is what he'd said. She was the daughter of a modern prostitute. She knew what the "and more" was.

Although he'd said he'd loved her.

But lots of men had told her mother they loved her. It was all to get one thing.

If Chandler actually loved her, he would have been talking about taking her with him, or staying with her, or marriage.

She'd been going to skip the ladies' meeting tonight, but she'd also bought a phone in the past two months, and Miss Lynette had texted her asking her if she was coming.

She probably should go even though she didn't feel like it.

There had been a couple of movies that she'd really enjoyed, not his romances, but his very first movie had been the best that he done in her opinion, and she'd watched it four times.

She'd been going to watch a fifth time tonight.

She checked her watch, still not used to having a phone she could just look at. She'd be late for the meeting, but she could make it.

She threw a skirt and a clean shirt on and checked her hair in the bathroom mirror. Grabbing her keys and wallet, she shoved aside the hurt and melancholy that had never left.

After watching all of Chandler's movies, she understood why he was so popular. He almost looked better onscreen than off.

She'd take his off-screen persona over his on-screen, any day. Except the romantic comedies. Those had been too real to be enjoyable.

Marlowe had brought her up to speed on using her phone and the Internet changes that had happened after she'd graduated from school, and she'd wasted more time than she wanted to admit finding out just how popular Chandler Hudson was.

No wonder he hadn't wanted to stay.

It had been two months. How long was she going to pine over him?

Getting out and doing things was supposed to help, but the hard part was actually doing it, because she didn't feel like doing anything except watching his movies over and over again.

With her hand on the doorknob, she yanked it open, determined she was going to put her month with Chandler out of her mind. If not completely out, at least file it under things that were fun, but over.

There was only one thing in that file.

It took two seconds for her to realize that Chandler was standing in her doorway with his hand raised to knock.

He looked just as surprised as she felt to see her yanking the door open before he touched it. It made her want to giggle. She didn't. His eyes looked her up and down; she was suddenly nervous. She hadn't realized before what a big movie star he was, and she was, frankly, intimidated.

She was glad she hadn't known when she bid on him, or she never would've done it.

Maybe just to humble him. And teach him a lesson. She never had figured out who had given her the money.

Not that it mattered. She was the one who'd been humbled.

She'd learned that she wasn't as different from her mother as she thought she was. In fact, she was just like every other woman in America who had a major crush on Chandler Hudson.

Although, the Chandler that she'd known, especially at the end of their month together, was completely different than the Chandler in the movies he made. She could almost see the progression of his change, from the first movie to the last.

They stood there staring at each other. She supposed it was her job to start the conversation since the house was hers.

"I can't think of what to say," she said. There. She talked.

"How about, Hi, Chandler," he said, his face completely serious.

"Hi, Chandler." She hadn't said his name out loud since the day he left. It felt good on her tongue.

"Hello, Ivory." His voice was a low rumble, and her hand tightened on the doorknob that she'd never let go of.

There wasn't a hint of smile on his face. "You could ask me in."

Hurt tumbled in her chest like leaves whipped by storm winds. The man in front of her, was the man on the screen. The same one she'd been watching for two months. But she'd never seen him look this insecure. It made her chest clench and loosened something in the tightness of her neck.

But her fear was stronger than her hope, and she said, "Why are you here?"

He flinched, just barely, but she saw it.

She shouldn't have said that. She'd been two months trying to get over him, hadn't been able to.

She thought that she'd been just like her mother, and the rest of the girls in the world. But now, she realized that maybe that thinking was wrong. Because she wasn't going from man to man to man depending on anyone who would have her.

It was only Chandler.

"Forget that. Please come in. It's good to see you. It's *very* good to see you."

She stepped back, opening the door wider, and wondering if, after her rather cold and awkward reception, it probably would be even more awkward for her to step forward and hug him now.

"If you don't want me here, I can leave."

"I do want you. I didn't want you to leave to begin with."

"You said something about a clean break?"

"I'm sorry. I thought it would be best. Easier isn't always better I guess." She wanted to reach for him, but held her hands out instead. "I'm so sorry. I shouldn't have been more concerned about what was going to hurt less and what...was going to make me less like my mother." She looked at the floor. That was the only way she could think of to describe it.

"I'm glad I wasn't the only one that was hurting." He hadn't moved from where he'd stood just outside the door. "You're the farthest thing from your mother." He spoke fiercely, but soft, and her head jerked up.

"No." She thought there would be pain. She hadn't realized how much pain. And she'd already figured out that loving one man didn't mean that she would fall into anyone's arms.

"I told you that I loved you. I just want you know that's still true. It's never going to change."

It wasn't hard to know what to say to that. "I love you too. I had no idea that love involves so much pain."

"We're a crazy pair, aren't we? I don't think it needs to be painful."

She had to smile. Because she thought he was right. "I guess we're just pretty good at making simple things complicated then? It's probably not a talent that's in high demand."

Her smile came easier. "Speaking of talent, I bought a TV and watched all of your movies." She wasn't going to tell him how many times she'd watched him. "You are talented."

He lifted his shoulder, shrugging, shaking his head. "No. That's not the kind of talent that matters. I mean, it's fun to entertain people, but it's more important to live a good life. I messed up when I left here. I should have taken more time."

"You had a hard blow." She hadn't even asked how he was, and she felt bad. She'd been inconsiderate, just thinking of herself and how much she'd been hurting. "Are you okay? How is RaeAnne?"

"We're fine. It was a crazy week until we got everything settled. Hollywood does everything big. And Las Vegas is just the same." He looked off into the distance and swallowed. "I think RaeAnne will be fine. She loved her mother. Obviously. And Jessica was a good mom." He nodded, looking back, as though needing to confirm that she agreed.

She had no idea what kind of mom Jessica was, but she nodded anyway, just to make him feel better.

"But it's a blur, because I wanted to be able to call you and talk to you and be with you, and as it was they delayed filming for me, and I had to get on set as soon as possible, and you don't have a phone."

She held up the phone that she'd bought since he left. "I do now." She weighed the phone back and forth.

"Looks like you're proud of that thing." He chuckled.

"It's fun. Addicting. I've definitely lost some work over it." Mostly googling him.

"It'll wear off some in a bit. You're right, though. It is addicting." His expression became serious.

They hadn't been talking about anything important, almost like they needed to find their footing with each other again, but his face said he had something he wanted her to know.

A little shot of fear sparked through her, tempered by the hope that had blossomed in her chest.

"I couldn't stop thinking about you." He lifted a hand like he was going to reach for her, but dropped it. "Couldn't stop thinking about being here. I've been discontent before, but I've never longed for a place, nor for a person, the way I long for you and this farm. I know I'm springing everything on you, after being gone for so long, although I would have called you every day if I'd have known that you had a phone," he gave her a lifted brow look, "and maybe we have some things to work out. But you just said you love me..."

She nodded. She wasn't taking it back.

"I know I've said in the past that I've tried marriage and it didn't work, but I think maybe I wasn't ready for it? Or maybe I wasn't serious about it." He sighed like the words were hard to say. "I'd like to be serious about it with you."

"Are you asking me to marry you?" It was about as a backhanded proposal she'd ever heard of if he was, which almost made her smile – he might play in rom-coms, but his real life technique maybe needed some work, except it didn't, because it only meant he didn't say things like this to every girl he dated.

"I guess I kinda was. Maybe I was just saying that I'm back here because I want to court you and would like get you to agree to marry me."

Her brows lifted. "Courting sounds fun. Old-fashioned, but fun."

"It seemed like it suited you. Although now you have a TV and phone, maybe we should just hook up."

"Or not. I'll take courting."

He laughed. "How long do you think this courting stuff will take?"

"Well if you'd asked me to marry you, I'd have said yes right now. But courting...a year?"

He dropped to a knee. "Will you marry me?"

Ivory froze. Was he serious?

No ring, no long, drawn-out declaration of love, just a simple question. She kind of liked simple. She was a simple person.

"Yes. I will."

"Just like that?" He said, his head tilted.

"Are you giving me a chance to change my mind?"

He stood, drawing her to him, and tilting his head. "No." Then his eyes narrowed. "Did you want to?"

In answer she reached up, slipping her arms around his neck, and tugging until he lowered his head. "No," she whispered as their lips finally met.

Epilogue

———

Deacon Hudson walked into church, the soothing environment wrapping around him and easing the burdens from his shoulders with just a few deep breaths.

Of all the places in the world, he loved God's house the best. He'd always felt at home here.

He was early for Sunday school, as always. It'd been his habit to come and pray before he got in the bus and drove the route to pick up kids for Sunday School.

He walked behind pews toward the center aisle when Miss Lynette came up the stairs from the basement. She seemed like she'd expected to see him.

"Deacon, I thought that was you. I wanted to see you for a moment?"

"Sure." Her words had been phrased as a question, but he wouldn't tell her no, and she probably knew it.

"You know Miss Inez. She lost her husband last fall?"

"Sure do. She's been going here for years." The church had done all kinds of fundraisers and gift baskets for her and her seven kids.

They'd bought gifts for the family for Christmas and Deacon actually mowed her yard every week.

Lynette had more on her mind, he was sure. He waited.

"I'm just going to come right out and say, I think that you and she would make a good pair. I'd like for you guys to meet and talk about it."

His stomach bounced up and hit his tonsils.

Okay. She'd surprised him.

Deacon shifted, looked over Miss Lynette's head at the cross hanging on the far wall of the church. It was empty. Of course. Just a plain wooden one. Not fancy in any way.

He stared, not really seeing the cross. Thinking about Tinsley. He'd never tried to find out who her mother was. He had never tried to find out who had given her to him, and written that note that had derailed everything he had planned for his life.

He wouldn't change it for the world though, wouldn't give up Tinsley for anything.

What seemed like a horrible awful thing at the time, had produced his daughter whom he loved more than anything in the world.

He still wondered, though, what exactly God had been thinking when He allowed it to happen.

"Deacon?" Miss Lynette interrupted his thoughts. His eyes turned back down to her.

"I was just thinking."

"I know seven kids is a lot —"

He held up his hand. "I love children." That was true. He hadn't really thought much about Inez.

Actually, he hadn't been thinking about her just now, either. Which probably didn't bode well for any type of relationship they might have.

"I don't want to push you, or make you do anything that you don't want to do. But she could really use a husband." Miss Lynette's lips turned up in a gentle smile. "I hate to see you alone. I think you'd be happier with a wife."

Deacon tried to keep his lips from flattening in irritation. She was probably right, and even if she wasn't, she was only trying to be helpful. But he didn't want just any wife, he wanted someone...

He didn't know. He just wanted God to bring someone into his life that he wouldn't be bored with. That challenged him, in a good way. He knew he was probably the kind of man people looked at and thought would want a good steady wife. A friend, lots of kids, boring.

He did want that. Maybe not the boring. He wanted a wife who was also a friend, but he wanted...excitement?

He couldn't disagree with Miss Lynette, though. He was lonely. Inez, with her seven children would certainly liven up his life.

God? Is this what You want from me? Is it You opening a door?

He really hoped it wasn't. But, maybe it would be for the best.

It felt like an open door, so he decided he'd walk through.

"Sure. I'll talk to her today. See if she wants to go somewhere and chat. Thanks for suggesting it."

He kind of felt like he should feel a little more excited, if this were truly the woman he was going to marry.

As if God knew exactly what he was thinking, the door opened and his brother Chandler walked in with Ivory. RaeAnne wasn't with them; she had stayed the night at their mom's house with Tinsley. They'd be along later.

But he wasn't really thinking about their children. He was looking at his brother as he looked at Ivory, almost a look of idolizing worship. Definitely a look of love. It was the way his dad still looked at his mom. It was the kind of look he wanted to give to his wife.

Ivory laughed at something Chandler said, and her hand went up and touched his arm. He noted the engagement ring on her finger. Blinking under the church lights.

Chandler probably could have afforded something much bigger, but Ivory wasn't a pretentious kind of woman, and he didn't think either one of them cared about diamonds or jewelry or anything like that. Especially since Chandler had retired from acting.

"Hey bro. Usually you're on your bus route right now. Running late?" Chandler asked, his hand going down and Ivory's slipping into it naturally, like they were so in tune with each other, they moved together.

He wanted that.

"Have you guys set a date yet?" It wasn't something he would normally care about, but he supposed with Miss Lynette's question, it was on his mind right now. He could be married next year this time. Tinsley would have a mom. And if it were Inez, he would have a whole house full of children.

He didn't mind that, necessarily. But the idea was foreign.

Ivory's cheeks turned a little pink, as Chandler looked down at her. Deacon might have had aspirations to be a pastor, but he was pretty sure what was going through their minds.

Finally Chandler looked up with a cocky grin. "I think we're going to have a small wedding in the next few weeks. No point in dragging things out."

That certainly made Deacon's brows go up.

"You gonna give us marriage counseling, bro?"

He snorted. "I don't think you'd take me seriously. You better talk to pastor."

"We already talked about it. We'd rather have you." Chandler was a serious as Deacon had ever seen him.

"Okay. Four sessions."

"Will you marry us?"

There was something in his chest that seemed to grow and expand, something warm and happy. "I sure will."

It would be a blessing to marry two people who were so obviously in love. It was the best five thousand dollars he'd ever spent.

———

Join Jessie's list and be the first to know about new releases and sales on her books!

Read My Dearest Blair, formerly titled *A Secret Baby in the Show Me State*, the next book in the Cowboy Crossing series. Deacon gets his story. A midnight tryst, an unknown admirer and a baby that is delivered to church with just a short note. Keep reading for a sneak peek now.

A Gift from Jessie

View this code through your smart phone camera to be taken to a page where you can download a FREE ebook when you sign up to get updates from Jessie Gussman! Find out why people say, "Jessie's is the only newsletter I open and read" and "You make my day brighter. Love, love, love reading your newsletters. I don't know where you find time to write books. You are so busy living life. A true blessing." and "I know from now on that I can't be drinking my morning coffee while reading your newsletter – I laughed so hard I sprayed it out all over the table!"

Claim your free book from Jessie!

Escape to more faith-filled romance series by Jessie Gussman!

The Complete Sweet Water, North Dakota Reading Order:

Series One: Sweet Water Ranch Western Cowboy Romance (11 book series)

Series Two: Coming Home to North Dakota (12 book series)

Series Three: Flyboys of Sweet Briar Ranch in North Dakota (13 book series)

Series Four: Sweet View Ranch Western Cowboy Romance (10 book series)

Spinoffs and More! Additional Series You'll Love:

Jessie's First Series: Sweet Haven Farm (4 book series)

Small-Town Romance: The Baxter Boys (5 book series)

Bad-Boy Sweet Romance: Richmond Rebels Sweet Romance (3 book series)

Sweet Water Spinoff: Cowboy Crossing (9 book series)

Small Town Romantic Comedy: Good Grief, Idaho (5 book series)

True Stories from Jessie's Farm: Stories from Jessie Gussman's Newsletter (3 book series)

Reader-Favorite! Sweet Beach Romance: Blueberry Beach (8 book series)

Blueberry Beach Spinoff: Strawberry Sands (10 book series)

From Strawberry Sands to: Raspberry Ridge (12 book series)

Swoonfully Jolly Holiday Stories:

Holiday Romance: Cowboy Mountain Christmas (6 book series)

Cowboy Mountain Christmas Spinoff: A Heartland Cowboy Christmas (9 book series)

New and Much Loved: Mistletoe Meadows (4 books and counting!)

Laughing Through the Snow: Christmas Tree, PA Sweet Romcoms (6 short reads)

www.ingramcontent.com/pod-product-compliance
Lightning Source LLC
Chambersburg PA
CBHW021357150726
47989CB00005B/2285